"What are you doing?" he growl

His voice h...
Marcy bega...   er.

"Phrenology...
about a pers... .... lumps and
protruberances."

"Now, that's a concept with some interesting
ramifications." He grabbed her around the
waist, pulling her over the back of the sofa.

"What are *you* doing?" Marcy demanded.

"This is what you said you wanted," he
murmured, pulling her against his chest.

"It is?"

"You told me to try being more spontaneous.
Normally," he continued in a conversational
tone, as though he weren't practically lying
on top of her, "when an attractive woman
starts running her fingers through my hair,
I restrain the impulse to grab her and kiss
her senseless."

"But?"

"But this time, I'm not going to."

Popular **Judith McWilliams** continues to delight her many fans with her lighthearted, amusing stories. In *Not My Baby!* she throws her heroine into a madcap family and a mistaken-identity plot, and lets the laughs land where they may. The author of nine Temptation novels, Judith will be publishing her first Harlequin Historical romance in early 1994. She and her husband make their home in Indiana.

NOT MY BABY!

JUDITH McWILLIAMS

Harlequin Books

TORONTO • NEW YORK • LONDON
AMSTERDAM • PARIS • SYDNEY • HAMBURG
STOCKHOLM • ATHENS • TOKYO • MILAN
MADRID • WARSAW • BUDAPEST • AUCKLAND

Published April 1993

ISBN 0-373-25540-3

NOT MY BABY!

1

" AREN'T YOU GOING to let me in? I know it's late, but I have good news!" Bill's whiny voice scraped across Marcy Handley's tired mind.

She suppressed her impulse to keep the door closed, reminding herself that she couldn't afford to offend him, at least not yet. So she plastered on her best, unflappable-psychologist-dealing-with-an-unreasonable-patient expression, released her door chain and stepped back, allowing him to enter her apartment.

She forced a smile and prepared herself to spend the next half an hour as a fascinated audience of one while Bill Sidney pontificated on his latest discovery.

"Why don't you sit down for a minute? I'm about done with my packing and I could use a short break. I'm planning to get an early start on my vacation in the morning," she added, delivering the hint, but not expecting it to do any good.

She was right. It didn't. Pushing her open suitcase to one end of the couch, Bill sank into the cushions. "Instead of gallivanting around the countryside enjoying yourself, you ought to stay here and concentrate on writing. The study you did on how a woman's appearance affects the way people perceive her would make a good book, especially while there's still interest in your results," he declared.

"Bill, I have been on two syndicated talk shows, written seven articles for national magazines and—"

"But—"

"And signed a very lucrative contract to write a version of the book aimed at the average working woman. Believe me, considering the amount of the advance the publishers paid, they are not about to lose interest."

"They paid you an advance on an unwritten book?" Bill's watery blue eyes began to gleam. "Do you mind if I ask how much?"

"Not if you don't mind if I don't answer."

"Now, now," Bill murmured in what he seemed to think was a soothing manner. "It's not as if I'm indulging in idle curiosity." He gave her a warm smile that made him look like an aging cherub.

Marcy eyed him uncertainly.

"I mean, considering our relationship and all," he persevered.

"Our relationship?" Marcy parroted. Had she somehow missed part of the conversation? "What relationship?"

"Why, you must know the high regard I have for your work and for you as a person...." His eyes slid the length of her body and it was all Marcy could do to suppress a shiver of distaste, even though there was nothing more than mild desire in that look. She'd had strangers on the street study her with more interest.

"I have never approved of this modern fashion of women being so slim," he continued. "I like a woman with a little meat on her bones. Like you."

"Meat on my bones!" Marcy sputtered. "I am not fat!"

"I didn't say you were," he assured her earnestly. "I said that you weren't slim, and I also said that I liked you like that."

As soon as this vacation was over she was going on a diet, Marcy thought grimly. He made her sound like some kind of Amazon, about to lead her troops into battle.

"I think we could be a perfect team," he continued.

"A team of draft horses, from the sound of it!"

"Why, I could even collaborate on your book," he added brightly, as if the idea had just occurred to him.

"Oh?" Marcy murmured noncommittally. So that was what this was all about. Her book. It was common knowledge in the Psychology Department that Bill's failure to publish had cost him a promotion last year, and if she wasn't mistaken, he would be up for tenure next time around. Maybe he'd decided the easiest way to solve his problem was to try to take credit for *her* work.

"You said you had news?" she inquired, trying to redirect the conversation.

"Yes, I do." He looked immensely pleased with himself. "I was in the faculty lounge after the lecture by that visiting professor from Australia this evening. I overheard Dr. Frey telling Jack Weblin that he's going to support your candidacy for the chair."

"He said that?" Marcy asked, shaken by the surge of excitement she felt. For once in his life, Bill was right. This was good news. Maybe even great news. Dr. Frey was one of the oldest and most respected members of her department. He was also one of the most conservative. The idea of having a woman as chair had caused him a great deal of concern, which he hadn't hesitated to express. If he offered his support, it could sway enough undecided votes to ensure her election. And once she was in the chair, she could begin to introduce some new ideas into the department. Such as making the education of students the number one priority instead of research.

"I don't doubt you're surprised at my news," Bill said smugly. "I must admit I rather expected him to vote for Joe Abernathy. I mean, Dr. Frey's always been such a staunch supporter of our retiring chair, and everyone knows that the two of you have had your differences. But Dr. Frey told Jack that he feels you are an example of what a college professor should be. He said he'd originally had some doubts about having a modern young woman in such a responsible position, but he'd finally decided that you are a credit to the university."

Marcy blinked at the unexpected accolade. "Coming from Dr. Frey, that's high praise indeed."

"I should think so." For a second, Bill looked distinctly peevish. "The best thing he ever said about me was that I didn't smoke. Now, about us . . ."

Marcy took a deep, steadying breath. She disliked hurting people's feelings, and it wasn't as if Bill was a nasty individual. He was simply a pompous bore, about as appealing as last week's rice pudding.

"Bill—" She broke off in relief as the doorbell rang again. Hopefully, the interruption would give her time to figure out how to turn Bill down without turning him into an enemy. She still needed his vote, but she wasn't willing to lie for it.

Marcy opened the door again. This time she found a very thin, teenage girl, dressed entirely in black. Her medium-length brown hair was disheveled, and she was clutching a black leather portfolio to her chest like a shield.

"Yes?" Marcy gave her a warm smile, trying to place her. She didn't think the girl lived in the apartment building, but there was something vaguely familiar about her.

"May I help you?" Marcy went on when the girl simply continued to stare at her, tension visible in every line of her body.

"Mmm…you…are you Marcy Handley?" she asked, her voice shaking.

"That's right." Marcy smiled again. "And you are?"

"I'm…I'm…I'm your daughter, Stephanie Brockton." Her huge brown eyes were fixed on Marcy's face with a desperate intensity.

Behind her she heard Bill Sidney gasp, adding to her sense of unreality.

She eyed the girl sympathetically. "I'm afraid you've made a mistake, my dear," she said gently.

"No!" Stephanie burst out.

"I am not your mother," Marcy repeated firmly. "I'm not anyone's mother. I may be a little absentminded at times, but I can guarantee you that I would never have forgotten having had a child." She tried to soften the blow. "Especially not one as pretty as you."

Stephanie gulped. "I know I don't look like you. I mean my hair's just plain brown instead of having that pretty reddish glow like yours does, but it doesn't matter what I look like. I've got proof."

"Well, really!" Bill was clearly in his element.

Marcy turned and looked at him. Of all the times for this girl to show up on her doorstep, it had to be when the university's biggest gossip was sitting in her living room! If Bill spread this around, it could damage her chances of being elected. Being a woman candidate was hard enough; being a woman with a past was something else again.

Stephanie spun around as if suddenly becoming aware of Bill's presence. "I'm sorry. I didn't . . . Are you married to my mother?" she asked.

"Certainly not!" Bill puffed out his chest like a pigeon. "I can see I was entirely mistaken in my assessment of your mother's character!" Getting to his feet, he marched out, slamming the door shut behind him.

Marcy let out her breath on a long sigh. Maybe by morning he would have calmed down enough for her to reason with him. At least this late at night there wouldn't be too many people awake with whom he could share his story.

"I'm so glad you're not married to him," Stephanie said hesitantly. "He'd make a terrible father."

"Be that as it may, the fact remains that I am not your mother. I am Marcy Handley, associate professor of psychology here at the university, and I have never been married."

"I know that. I also know that you promised you'd never contact me again after the adoption. But don't you see?" Stephanie pleaded. "It doesn't matter anymore. My mom and dad died in a plane crash five months ago. They can't be hurt by your telling me the truth now."

"Stephanie, I am telling you the truth."

"Here." Stephanie shoved the portfolio she was carrying at her. "Read this and you'll see that there's no reason for you to continue to lie to me. I already know everything."

"Lovely. And I don't know anything." Marcy took the document case.

"Read it. Please," Stephanie urged.

Marcy sank onto the couch beside her suitcase, opened the file and began to read. As Stephanie had claimed, it contained all of the records of her adoption, which had been handled privately by a law firm in New York City. The further Marcy read, the more confused she became. Someone with her name was indeed listed as Stephanie's birth mother, but the copies of the birth mother's social security card, birth certificate, baptismal record and confirmation papers were what really raised the hair on the back of Marcy's neck. They were definitely hers.

Marcy frowned at the wall opposite. This whole thing made no sense. While she was supposed to have been giving birth to this teenager sitting across from her, looking for all the world like a puppy begging to be taken in and given a home, she had in fact been a freshman at Stanford University in California. And while she was perfectly willing to believe that there was more than one Marcy Handley in the world, she knew very well that there was only one with her social security number and birth certificate.

Marcy held the copy of the surrender of custody form that the birth mother had signed close to the lamp and studied the signature. It definitely wasn't hers. And it didn't look as if someone had tried to copy the way she normally signed her name. Nor was the handwriting familiar.

She glanced speculatively at Stephanie. "Tell me, where do you live now?"

Stephanie grimaced. "With my Uncle Paul. Mom's brother."

"And this Uncle Paul just let you come to see me?"

"Well..." The girl fiddled with the strap of her purse. "Not exactly."

"Well, what exactly?"

"I didn't tell him I was coming," she said. "He thought I was going to school when I left the house this morning. I did leave him a note, though. He probably got it when he got home from work."

"And you don't think he might be worried about you?"

"Maybe a little," she admitted. "But he wouldn't have let me come if I'd told him about it beforehand."

"Probably not. The poor man must be frantic. Give me his phone number, and I'll call him."

"No! It isn't as if he really knows me. Or cares about me. I'm just a duty he inherited. He never even mentions my mom and dad and he never seems to know what to say to me." Stephanie's lower lip quivered.

A common enough problem among adults dealing with teenagers, Marcy thought, her sympathies now divided equally between Stephanie and her uncle.

"Not only that, but he's a stuffy old bachelor," Stephanie added.

Marcy stared at the girl for a moment, seeking further enlightenment. When none was forthcoming, she finally asked, "Stuffy old bachelors aren't supposed to worry?"

"You don't understand," Stephanie cried. "You're my mother! How can you not understand?" she went on, promptly bursting into loud, hiccuping sobs.

Marcy diagnosed incipient hysteria. Obviously, Stephanie had screwed up her courage to take this step, and now that the reality wasn't living up to her fantasy, she just couldn't take it.

"Calm down, Stephanie," Marcy soothed. "I have a very old, very nosy neighbor across the hall who'll think I'm beating you."

A tiny, watery chuckle escaped Stephanie. "She sounds like my Aunt Clementia."

"Would you like me to call your Aunt Clementia instead of your uncle?" Marcy asked.

"No! Aunt Clementia is old. Mom always said we shouldn't worry her."

"All right. No Aunt Clementia. But there must be someone who—"

"If you don't want me, then I'm going to run away to California!" Stephanie burst into tears again.

"The last flight left our local airport over an hour ago," Marcy said matter-of-factly. "And believe me, you wouldn't enjoy a cross-country bus trip, even if you could get a bus at this hour. Why don't you spend the night here with me and we can discuss the situation in the morning, when we're both feeling a little more rested?"

"I can stay here with you?" Stephanie's face lit up.

"You can stay the night," Marcy repeated, doing her best not to show her very real pity for the girl. Stephanie didn't need pity. What she needed—what they both needed—was some help in sorting out this mess. And what a mess it was. How had she, Marcy Handley, ever come to be listed as this girl's mother?

"Oh, thank you for letting me stay!" Stephanie flung her arms around Marcy. "Where can I sleep?" She glanced brightly around the small, cluttered living room.

"You can have the bedroom," Marcy said, resigning herself to a night on the couch. If Stephanie should change her mind during the night and try to sneak out, Marcy would have a chance to stop her. She shuddered at the thought of what might happen to a young, vulnerable girl wandering around the streets at night. Even their sleepy little Indiana college town had had its share of rapes and murders.

"It'll be just like a slumber party," Stephanie enthused. "We can talk and—"

"No, it'll be like a good night's sleep," Marcy cut in. "There's only one bed in there. I'll spend the night out here on the couch."

"Oh." Stephanie's face fell, and Marcy felt a pang of guilt, which she ignored. She would not be doing Stephanie any favors by encouraging her in the mistaken belief that she was her mother. It was essential for Stephanie to face the fact that what she'd built up in her mind was a fantasy. A fantasy. Although those papers . . .

But tomorrow was soon enough to worry about them. Right now sleep took priority.

"The bedroom is through there," she said briskly, pointing to the door in the far wall. "And the bath is across the hall. Go on to bed. I'll be turning in myself in a few minutes."

She began to close her suitcase, breathing a sigh of relief when she heard the sound of Stephanie's foot-

steps. Hopefully, by morning, the youngster would be
in a more reasonable frame of mind and would tell her
how to contact her uncle. Without knowing his last
name and the city where he lived, finding him would
be impossible. She could, of course, contact the police
for help, but didn't want to do that unless she absolutely had to. They would undoubtedly place Stephanie in protective custody, something guaranteed to
make her even more resentful. And that, in turn, would
be just one more obstacle for the unknown uncle to
overcome. Marcy felt a pang of empathy for Stephanie's uncle, but given the alternatives, letting him worry
for one night seemed the lesser evil.

MARCY FELT as if she had just fallen asleep, after tossing and turning for what had seemed like hours, when
the doorbell sounded. It rang several times before she
was able to realize that the sound she was hearing
wasn't part of her dream.

Not awake enough to remember where she was, she
stumbled off the couch and bashed one leg on a corner
of the coffee table.

"Damn!" she muttered, hopping toward the door on
her undamaged leg.

Checking to make sure the chain was still on, she
opened the door a fraction.

After the darkness of her apartment, the bright light
from the hall hurt her eyes. She squinted, trying to clear
her vision and found herself staring at a navy-and-red-
striped tie. It was slightly askew, giving her a clear view

of buttons marching up the front of a starched white dress shirt.

Her gaze followed the row of buttons, pausing when she came to a tanned neck, whose tendons stood out in stark relief, which gave her some idea of the tension the man was under. Her eyes drifted higher, over tightly clenched jaws. A swarthy haze of emerging beard further darkened an already dark skin, giving the stranger a faintly piratical look that was enhanced by the jut of high cheekbones and the sharp blade of the nose. Marcy went on looking, then frowned when she saw the emotion swirling in the man's coal black eyes.

Fear, she concluded. But why? She frowned again, remembering the strange end of her evening. Of course. This apprehensive-looking man must be Stephanie's "stuffy old" uncle.

"Uncle Paul, I presume?" she inquired, wanting to make sure of the man's identity before she invited him inside.

The relief that swept over his face was all the answer she needed.

"Stephanie's safe?" he demanded.

"Yes." Marcy released the chain and stepped aside to allow him to enter. "She's asleep." She flipped on the overhead lights, but was a fraction of a second too late. Uncle Paul, not seeing Marcy's suitcase on the floor, tripped over it, landing on his hands and knees.

Marcy listened to his muttered stream of curses in awe as she stared down at him. Despite her attempt to suppress it, a smile lifted her lips. This was the first time she could ever remember having had a man literally at her feet.

"Did you hurt anything?" She kept her voice even with an effort.

"My dignity," he said dryly. "Tell me, do you always store your suitcases in the middle of the room?" He got to his feet and brushed at the knife-edge creases in his pants.

She chuckled. "Invariably. It's a marvelous deterrent to burglars."

"She really is safe?" he asked suddenly, almost as if afraid to believe it.

"Physically, she's fine. Mentally, she seems to be a bit distracted," Marcy said carefully.

"She's not the only one." He shoved his fingers through his hair. "When I found out she'd taken off on some harebrained quest to find you..." A tremor chased over his features.

"Worrying about what might have happened is pointless. Nothing did," Marcy said practically. "Would you like a drink?"

"A stiff shot of whiskey, if you've got it." He sank onto her sofa, stretched his long legs in front of him and leaned his head against the cushion. He looked exhausted, both physically and emotionally.

Stephanie was wrong about her uncle, Marcy thought as she poured him a snifter of her prize fifty-year-old brandy. He obviously cared about her. However, Marcy wasn't certain *why*. Did he love her? Or was he just worrying about what his friends might say about her running away?

Paul opened his eyes to find himself being studied and felt a flash of anger. How could Stephanie have done this? Why had she gone searching for this woman, after all he'd tried to do? This woman had never shown the slightest interest in her, after all.

He made an effort to suppress his anger and accepted the drink. "You are Marcy Handley, Stephanie's biological mother, aren't you?" He realized belatedly that they hadn't introduced themselves.

"Yes and no."

He frowned at her. "Listen, lady, it's the middle of the night. A night I've spent in a state of panic, worrying about what might have happened to my niece. And on top of that, I've just flown halfway across the country. I am not operating at my peak mental capacity. Try being a little less inscrutable."

"Yes, I am Marcy Handley. No, I am not Stephanie's mother."

"I know you aren't her mother," he said tightly. "At least not in any way that counts. My sister Hillary was. Hillary was the one who took her home from the hospital and walked the floor with her nights. Who fed her and loved her and worried over her. Not you."

He got to his feet and began to pace, too upset to sit still. "I know it isn't your fault that Stephanie decided to track you down, but you must see that it will never do for her to get friendly with you."

"Actually, no. I don't see why it's automatically a bad idea for her to get to know her mother."

"I told you! My sister was her mother! A mother isn't like a car. You don't run out and replace it when something happens to the first one."

"Not replace it." Marcy wanted to give him some inkling of what the girl was probably feeling. "One never really replaces something that is loved, whether it's a person or a pet. But that doesn't mean you can't form other relationships with other people who can meet your emotional needs."

"She doesn't need you! She has me," he insisted. "I can take care of Hillary's daughter."

Marcy resisted the urge to point out that he didn't seem to have done such a great job thus far. "Hillary's daughter's name is Stephanie," she said finally.

"I know that a damn sight better than you do." He took a quick gulp of the whiskey. "Hillary said they offered to let you name her, but you said you didn't want any part of it."

"*I* didn't say anything, because I'm not Stephanie's mother."

A wail of anguish came from the now-open bedroom door. "How can you deny me? What's wrong with me that my own mother won't even acknowledge me?"

"Stephanie," Paul said tightly, "my sister was your mother."

"And I loved her." Marcy saw Stephanie's eyes fill with tears. "But she's gone now and..." The girl turned to Marcy as if unsure of what to call her. "And you're my mother, too."

"No, I'm not," Marcy repeated for what seemed like the hundredth time. "Someone has made one gigantic mistake in those records."

"Don't say that," Stephanie moaned. "I already love you."

Marcy sighed. The pain this pair was feeling was almost tangible. Her frustration at not being able to produce an answer that would ease their pain was acute.

Fate had shattered Stephanie's previously secure world, and she was desperately seeking something or someone to magically make everything right for her again. And who could do that better than her birth mother, however much she'd loved her adoptive mother?

"Please let me stay with you," Stephanie begged. "Once you get to know me you'll see that I can be a really great daughter. Truly I can."

"I'm sure you are a great daughter," Marcy said emphatically. "You simply aren't *my* great daughter, and that fact must be faced."

"The papers in my folder say I am," Stephanie insisted.

Marcy tried another tack. "Stephanie, even if I wanted to invite you to stay with me, I couldn't. It's the middle of September. You must be in school by now. I'm about to leave on vacation."

"You can spend your vacation with us. Can't she, Uncle Paul?" Stephanie turned to him pleadingly.

Paul focused on Marcy, taking a good look at her for the first time. She couldn't be more than five-four even in those thick, fuzzy socks she was wearing. His eyes strayed upward, over the well-worn sweatpants that molded her full hips and the thin cotton T-shirt that faithfully outlined her large breasts.

"Please, Uncle Paul, how can you deny me the right to know my own mother?" Stephanie demanded. "If you don't let her come, I'll hate you forever."

"Stephanie, be reasonable." Paul shoved his fingers through his hair. Why would she want to invite a total stranger into their home? Especially when the woman wouldn't even admit that she was the girl's mother.

"I'll run away to California! I'll flunk out of school! I'll . . ." Stephanie's voice rose hysterically.

"Would you consider behaving?" Paul muttered.

"Will you let my mother come and visit me?" Stephanie countered.

"My sister was your mother!" Paul bit out from the depths of his grief. "You don't even know this woman!"

"And I won't ever get a chance to if you have your way!"

Paul clenched his teeth, wishing that Stephanie were simply young enough to be picked up and physically removed from the scene. But the very thought of trying to drag a kicking, screaming fifteen-year-old through an airport was too much, even for his sangfroid.

Then his sense of justice nudged inside the hurt, anger and jealousy long enough for him to admit that

Stephanie might have a point. If this Marcy Handley really was her birth mother, did he have the moral right to refuse them the opportunity to get to know each other? But if he did invite this woman into his home, what might be the result? Nobody knew better than he that his relationship with Stephanie was shaky, at best. How could it grow into anything more substantial if Stephanie invested all her emotions into getting to know this woman instead of himself?

But what would happen if he refused to invite her? Stephanie would blame him, and their relationship would really be on the rocks. He stifled a sigh. *You're damned if you do and damned if you don't....*

He shot the silent Marcy a speculative glance. Why had she denied the relationship? Could Stephanie somehow have her facts wrong? Was there a man in Marcy's life who wouldn't approve of her having had a child out of wedlock? Did she simply not want to deal with the past? Maybe she'd turn down an invitation. He felt a glimmer of hope. That way he could appear to be giving Stephanie what she thought she wanted, without further damaging their relationship. He decided to risk it.

Turning to Marcy, he said, "All right, you can come for a visit."

Marcy barely heard Stephanie's whoop of joy as she studied Paul's tense features. She had no illusions about what he was hoping for. For a second she was tempted to simply give him what he wanted and send both them and their problems away, but she couldn't quite bring

herself to do it. She'd built her whole life around helping people, and if ever there were two people who
needed help . . .

But there was also the question of how her name had
come to be on those adoption papers. Someone had
deliberately used her identity, and Marcy wanted,
needed, to know who and why. Quickly. Otherwise,
she might lose some of that hard-won support for the
upcoming election.

Feeling as if she were about to take a big step into the
unknown, Marcy smiled gently at Stephanie and said,
"For a visit, then."

2

"I ASSURE YOU, Dr. Frey, the young girl in question is not my daughter." Fighting to keep the anger and frustration out of her voice, Marcy glared at her living-room wall.

"If you say so." He sounded skeptical.

"I absolutely and positively say so. I do not, nor have I ever had a daughter. Or a son, for that matter." Marcy spoke with all the sincerity she could muster. "This is simply a case of a young girl seeking her birth mother and not having the resources to do it properly."

"But Bill Sidney said . . ."

"Damn Bill Sidney and his malicious gossip! Bill was . . . upset when the girl arrived."

"Any right-thinking person would be."

Sanctimonious old twit, Marcy thought, taking care to let none of her outrage be heard when she spoke again. "Oh, not about that." She paused deliberately, hoping to give the impression that she was trying to decide how much to reveal. "He was upset when I told him I wasn't interested in collaborating with him on my upcoming book. Or on anything of a more...personal nature."

"Oh." Dr. Frey suddenly sounded knowing. "That would explain it. Normally, of course, I wouldn't dream of prying into your private life, but with you in contention for the department chair . . . You must see that I'm very concerned that we elect a person who will project a positive image of the Psychology Department."

"Certainly. I understand your concern. And I do appreciate your calling me to find out the truth, instead of listening to gossip, as some people might. If I can be of any further help, please feel free to call me when I get back from my vacation. Goodbye, Dr. Frey."

Marcy gently replaced the receiver, though she really wanted to slam it down.

"Why me, Lord?" she demanded. "I lead a good life. I pay my bills on time. I'm nice to small children, dumb animals and even dumber adults. I've worked hard to get this promotion, and now, when it's almost mine, this happens."

How thoroughly Bill Sidney had spread the story! How conservative so many of her colleagues were!

She absolutely had to find out who Stephanie's mother was—and she had to do it fast. Perhaps her own mother would have some ideas. Marcy picked up the phone again and punched in her parents' number. Cradling the receiver against her left ear, she took a gulp of cold coffee.

"Mom?" She swallowed hurriedly and shifted the receiver. "Hi, it's me. I need help. Does the name Stephanie Brockton mean anything to you?"

"No, dear. I can't remember any Brocktons."

"Well, then, do you remember me at eighteen?"

"Certainly," Mrs. Handley replied promptly. "Pretty as a Gainsborough painting, valedictorian of your high school class, homecoming queen, third in the state in the hundred-meter butterfly stroke, and you knitted your father a green sweater for Christmas. He still wears it for gardening in the spring. And you were madly in love with that Chalmers boy. He's a pediatrician with two kids of his own now, you know." Marcy thought she heard faint regret in her mother's voice.

"Very impressive, Mom. Tell me, do your memories include me having a child?"

"Not that I recall, dear. Why do you ask?"

"Because last night a fifteen-year-old named Stephanie Brockton showed up on my doorstep, claiming that I'm her mother."

Mrs. Handley giggled engagingly. "The most fascinating things always seem to happen to you. So tell me all about my grandchild."

"You and I have very different definitions of what constitutes fascinating, Mom, and she most definitely isn't your grandchild, because I sure as hell didn't have her and I'm an only child."

"Couldn't we just keep her?" Mrs. Handley asked wistfully. "It'd be so nice to have a grandchild to brag about at the bridge club meetings. What does she look like?"

"Worrisome," Marcy said slowly.

"You mean like when you were sixteen and into your black-leather phase? I was so worried you were going to join a motorcycle gang that summer and ride off into the sunset."

"No, it's not how she dresses. It's how she looks. Like . . . like when we drag out all the old family pictures at Christmas, and if you squint at a photo of Great-grandmother Mostlinger, it looks a lot like me?"

"Hmm. I take it this Stephanie looks like the family, but not like anyone in particular."

"Exactly."

"Did she say why she settled on you as her mother?"

"Because the adoption records she apparently found among her parents' papers list one Marcy Handley as her mother."

"But even a fifteen-year-old must realize that there could be lots of Marcy Handleys in the United States."

"Not with my social security number, my birth certificate, my baptismal certificate and my confirmation certificate."

"Hmm. Let me think. Fifteen years ago all those papers would have been kept in your father's desk in his study."

"I know. It doesn't make any sense!" Marcy exclaimed in frustration. "Whoever used my name when Stephanie was born had to have had those documents."

"Perhaps they wrote to the state and the church and asked for duplicates? I saw a mystery show the other day on television where the villain took names off tombstones and created fake identities that way."

"But I'm not dead!" Marcy wailed. "Although I do feel like I'm in the middle of a hideous nightmare. The poor kid kept insisting that I was her mother and wouldn't listen to a word I said. And her uncle thought—"

"Uncle?" Mrs. Handley's voice sharpened. "He came with her?"

"He came *after* her, worried out of his mind and completely mishandling the situation. He has no more idea of how to relate to a teenager than the man in the moon."

"A bachelor, I take it?" The casually put question didn't fool Marcy for a minute. Her mother was an incorrigible matchmaker.

"Yes, according to Stephanie, he's a stuffy old bachelor." Marcy kept her own opinion to herself. The less her mother knew about Paul, the better.

"Oh." Mrs. Handley sounded disappointed. "An *old* bachelor. Stuffy you can change, old you can't."

"Not only that, but Bill Sidney was here when Stephanie arrived. You know what a gossip he is."

"You poor dear," her mother sympathized. "If I believed in fate, I'd tell you to go to bed and stay there, because someone up there certainly seems to have it in for you."

Marcy heaved a sigh. "To put it mildly. I've spent the morning fielding calls from members of the psychology department, telling me that the new chairperson, if it's a woman, must be above reproach."

"Man, thy name is hypocrisy."

"You'd better believe it. If I can't clear this whole mess up quickly, there's a good chance they'll elect Joe Abernathy instead of me. And to make matters worse, it'll probably be another twenty years before the job falls vacant again."

"When is the vote?"

"In three and a half weeks at the regular October meeting."

"Would it bother you that much to be passed over?"

"Yes," Marcy stated flatly. "I deserve that job. I've paid my dues by doing a lot of the donkey work for Dr. Wharton these past two years. Not only that, I honestly believe I'm the best—if you'll pardon the expression—man for the job. There are so many things that need to be done to make the department more responsible to the students' needs, but all Joe Abernathy cares about is how much research is produced by the professors. Just like Dr. Wharton."

"So what's your plan of action?" Mrs. Handley asked.

"First I'm going to visit Stephanie in Boston to see if I can find out anything about her biological mother. And I was wondering if you remembered anything going on in the family sixteen years ago that might shed some light on all of this."

"That was the year your Grandfather Handley died. We all spent a lot of time at the hospital with him toward the end. I vaguely remember your Aunt Eileen complaining one night about all the trouble Pam was causing with her willful ways, but I didn't really pay much attention, because your Aunt Eileen considers any behavior that she hasn't previously okayed willful. Thinking back on it, though, I can't remember having seen Pam at any of the family gatherings that winter. Not that there were all that many."

"If Pam had been pregnant, that would explain why she wasn't there," Marcy said slowly.

"But why use your identification if her parents already knew?"

"Perhaps the baby's father didn't? Maybe she had a premonition something like this would happen and wanted to protect herself," Marcy suggested. "When I get to Boston, I'm going to go through that adoption file with a fine-tooth comb. There might be a letter or a picture or something that'll have more significance for me than it had for Stephanie."

"Possibly. At any rate, I definitely think you ought to go to Boston and try to get to the bottom of this," Mrs. Handley said. "It's one thing to lose out on a job you really want to someone who's better qualified. It's quite another to lose out to innuendo and rumors spread by small-minded gossips like Bill Sidney."

"I'll say," Marcy muttered.

"And while you're investigating things in Boston, I'll give Pam a call and see what I can find out. I can also call your Grandmother Handley. She may be ninety-three, but she's sharp as a tack. Maybe she knows something about all this."

"Thanks, Mom. I appreciate it." Marcy slowly hung up the phone. Grandmother Handley would be an excellent source of information. She knew everything worth knowing about the family.

A chime from the clock on the desk reminded Marcy that she had less than an hour to finish packing and get to the airport if she was going to catch her plane.

She made it, barely. Almost as if to compensate for the traumatic events that had preceded it, her flight was totally uneventful. The weather was perfect all the way, her flight was right on schedule, and she made her connection to Boston without incident.

MARCY RELEASED HER BREATH on a long sigh when the airplane's wheels touched the runway at Logan Airport, and made a conscious effort to relax her tense muscles. No matter how often she flew, she could never quite shake a feeling of impending disaster.

Once the plane had safely docked and the passengers were allowed to depart, the man in the seat beside Marcy got to his feet. She followed suit and retrieved her briefcase from the overhead compartment, barely noticing the jabs and shoves she was receiving from the passengers behind her.

"Excuse me, but I have a connection to make and I'm already late." The speaker squeezed by.

Me too, Marcy thought, feeling an odd twist in her stomach. Hers was a very strange connection with an even stranger situation.

Paul had called earlier that morning to find out when she'd be arriving, and he'd told her that she would be met. Emerging from the tunnel into the terminal, she wondered if it would be Paul. Or why she wanted it to be Paul.

Marcy surveyed the people milling around. To her left, carefully scanning the disembarking passengers, was a family group. Directly in front of her, a middle-aged woman was rapturously hugging a howling infant, while its obviously besotted parents beamed.

Marcy stepped around the family, trying to get a better view of the crowd, disappointed not to see Paul's broad shoulders and dark head. She sank onto a plastic seat that felt every bit as uncomfortable as it looked. She'd give him fifteen minutes and then she'd take a cab to the address he'd given her, she decided. Hopefully, someone would be there. Maybe Aunt Clementia.

Marcy smiled, then grimaced. If only she knew a little more about these people! As it was, she knew only that she was not Stephanie's mother, and that neither Paul nor Stephanie believed her. Along with three-quarters of her colleagues in the Psychology Department, she reflected gloomily.

Determinedly shaking off her frustration, Marcy scanned the crowd again. Her heart skipped a beat; there was Paul's dark head! He was weaving his way through the crowded concourse, and suddenly she found herself standing on tiptoe to get a better look. He was wearing an impeccably tailored gray suit, teamed with a stark white shirt and conservative tie.

Marcy studied him carefully as he sidestepped a woman pulling a loaded luggage trolly with the lithe grace of a natural athlete. What did he do for a living? she wondered. Whatever it was, he seemed to have read the masculine equivalent of her study on dressing for maximum effect. The effects in his case were power and authority. They clung to him like a second skin.

She looked up as he reached her, taking in the social smile that was nothing more than a polite stretching of his facial muscles. What would he look like if he really smiled?

He reached down and picked up her suitcase. "Welcome to Boston," he said formally. "I hope you had an uneventful flight."

"Yes, thank you, Mr.... What is your last name, anyway?"

He studied her for a long moment, then said, "My sister never mentioned it?"

"Since I am not Stephanie's mother, I never had the opportunity to meet your sister. Your last name is...?" she persisted, falling into step beside him.

"Wycoff."

Wycoff? Marcy tried it out in her mind. Paul Wycoff. It suited him. "I take it Stephanie is in school?" she asked.

"Yes. She has a piano lesson today. Hillary felt she had a great deal of talent, which should be developed."

"Definitely not my child," Marcy murmured.

"You aren't musically inclined?" He motioned toward the door that led to the parking lot.

"I don't have even a smidgen of talent. My mother insisted I take piano lessons for three years, until my father finally said enough was enough."

Paul gave her a quick smile, and the corners of his eyes crinkled enticingly. "I know exactly what you mean. The piano was my parents' preferred instrument of torture, too."

"I don't know what it is about pianos that puts visions of Paderewski into the heads of otherwise perfectly normal parents," Marcy mused. "I swear, if I ever have any children, I'm going to banish all musical instruments from the house."

Paul stopped beside a shiny black Mercedes-Benz. "This is mine." Unlocking the door, he held it open for her.

Marcy sat down on the front seat and felt the soft glove leather curve lovingly around her hips. Intrigued, she studied the dashboard. It bore only a superficial resemblance to the one in her subcompact. Twisting slightly, she watched Paul put her case into the trunk, then get into the car. He carefully backed out of the narrow parking space.

"Now, then, Ms. Handley," he said, once he'd maneuvered the car into the heavy stream of traffic.

"Marcy will do."

"Marcy," he repeated. "What do you do at the university?"

"I teach psychology."

"Psychology!" He shot her a startled glance. "You mean like Freud, and having socially unacceptable thoughts about your mother?"

"No, I mean like understanding why people act the way they do."

"That'd be a neat trick. Most of the people I know don't seem to have the vaguest idea why they behave like they do."

"Very few people act completely spontaneously. There's usually a reason for any action, but I will admit that quite often the person isn't aware of it."

"Unaware sounds more like my behavior." He sighed despondently, and the sound gave Marcy an inkling of the pressure he must be under. "I honestly thought Stephanie was adjusting to her parents' death. I've been very careful not to talk about them and reopen the wounds."

"Bad idea," Marcy said. "By not talking about them you are, in effect, denying that they existed, which further adds to her sense of loss."

Paul grimaced. "Chalk up one more mistake to good intentions. I simply don't have any experience with kids. Nor do I really know Stephanie as a person all that well. But dammit all, she's my niece, and Hillary trusted me to raise her as she would have done. I've tried to make sure that everything has stayed the same. All the lessons. All the rules."

"Maintaining Stephanie's normal schedule is okay up to a point. But only to a point. Things aren't the same," Marcy said seriously. "You aren't Hillary. You're you. You wouldn't raise a child exactly the way your sister would, and trying to second-guess what she would have done in a given situation is bound to be adding tension to an already tense situation."

"I promised Hillary," he insisted doggedly. "Anyway, when I got home from work yesterday, I found that Stephanie had jimmied the lock to my desk, pilfered the adoption file and taken off across the country to find you."

"How did she know where to locate me?" Marcy asked. The question had been nagging at her.

"She said she called the church where you were confirmed, told them she was an old school friend and asked if they knew your address. They told her you worked at the university, and from there it was just a matter of looking you up in the phone book.

"For me it involved a frantic dash to the airport to charter a plane, all the time worried sick about what might happen to a naive, vulnerable fifteen-year-old."

So that was how he'd gotten into and out of their small town last night. "Your niece seems to be a very resourceful young lady."

"Yes. Actually, on the flight back home I read that file she took."

Marcy frowned. "You hadn't read it until then?"

"No. I was studying economics at Oxford the year she was adopted, so I didn't know any of the specifics. Besides, it didn't really matter. Stephanie was Hillary and David's daughter. What difference did it make where she came from?"

"Apparently to Stephanie it mattered quite a bit."

"So I discovered. At any rate, I'm willing to admit that you are her birth mother. However, according to my lawyer, you have absolutely no standing in a court of law. Hillary and David entrusted her to me and with me she stays."

"You're wrong."

"My lawyer says—"

"Not about that. About me being her mother. I've already told you that I'm not anyone's mother." Marcy had to struggle to keep her voice level. She was beginning to have a great deal of sympathy for Cassandra, the prophetess who had been cursed to always tell the truth and never to be believed.

He frowned. "Are you saying that those records are forgeries?"

"I don't know. They looked real. And no, I can't explain them." *Not yet*, she added silently. "But I don't care if the archangel Gabriel comes down and says she's mine, it isn't true."

Paul looked at her pityingly. Poor woman. Obviously someone in her past had made her feel so guilty about having had an illegitimate child that she now refused to even acknowledge the fact. He frowned thoughtfully. Or was she playing some deep game of her own? If so, what could her motive possibly be? He didn't know. He had to admit that he didn't know much about Marcy Handley at all.

He pressed his lips together in frustration. If only he had that report from the detective agency! Until he received it, he had no option but to allow Marcy Handley to enter his home; he certainly didn't want to run the risk of Stephanie leaving him again. Her rejection had left a bitter taste. How could she have cast aside everything he'd done for her these past five months to go chasing after a stranger? A stranger who hadn't wanted her fifteen years ago and didn't seem to want her now.

On the other hand, maybe taking this tack would work out for the best. Maybe once Stephanie saw that Marcy Handley didn't intend to admit to being her mother, she'd give up chasing after a will-o'-the-wisp and focus on the person who did want her. Himself. Then maybe they could try to forge a new family from the remnants of what had been. He shot Marcy a quick glance. What did she hope to gain by coming here? He found no answers in her face; all it reflected was polite interest.

Marcy climbed out of the Mercedes after he'd parked and turned to study the rambling, two-story colonial-style building. A curious sense of homecoming stole over her. Its white clapboard siding gleamed in the afternoon sunlight, and what seemed like acres of immaculately groomed lawn stretched from the black wrought-iron fencing at the sidewalk's edge to a stand of towering maple trees about six hundred feet behind the house. There was an aura about the house that could only come from years of loving care.

She turned and surreptitiously studied Paul, who was getting her luggage out of the trunk. Exactly who was he, and what did he do for a living to be able to afford a place like this?

"What's the matter?" he asked, slamming the trunk lid.

"I was wondering what you did for a living," she answered honestly. She'd learned long ago that the quickest and surest way to find out something was usually to ask.

He gave her a long, thoughtful look, then said, "I'm in investing."

"As in investing money?" She fell into step beside him.

"Yes." He set down her suitcases in front of the enormous black door and reached into his pants pocket.

Marcy watched his long fingers disappear from view. She narrowed her eyes as the movement tightened the gray fabric across his muscular thighs. She blinked to break the spell and asked, "Your money or other people's?"

"Both." His hand reappeared with a key, which he inserted into the polished brass lock. It turned with a well-oiled click. Most things in his life probably worked like that, Marcy reflected. Paul Wycoff had the air of a man who planned his life down to the last detail and tolerated no deviation from those plans. That was probably why he was having so much trouble with Stephanie. After all, the only thing predictable about teenagers was that they were unpredictable.

"You work in a bank?" she inquired.

"I own an investment firm." He pushed the door open and set her suitcase inside. "Caleb Wycoff founded it in 1679 with money he accumulated during his career as a pirate in the Caribbean."

A pirate? Marcy studied Paul's sharply chiseled features. She didn't need to stretch her imagination to see the pirate ancestor in Paul, who was now leaning against the antique table at one side of the huge entrance while he checked the answering machine for messages.

Still curious, Marcy looked around, blinking as diamond shards of light from the exquisite chandelier that hung from the ceiling two stories above bounced off the gleaming inlaid parquet floor.

"You're really here!" The youthful shriek came from Marcy's left, and she turned to see Stephanie emerge from what appeared to be the living room.

"I was so afraid you'd change your mind about coming to see me!" she exclaimed, her words tugging at Marcy's soft heart.

"Why aren't you at your piano lesson?" Paul demanded.

Stephanie glared at him. "Because I'm here."

Marcy saw Paul's lips tighten at the girl's flip answer. "I told you—"

"And I told the piano teacher that my mother was coming to visit me today," Stephanie retorted defiantly.

"Stephanie—" Marcy began, only to be interrupted by Paul.

"My sister was your mother!" The words were full of pain.

"And I loved her, but I hate you!" Stephanie yelled. "I wish you'd been the one who'd died instead of her!" She ran past him and pounded up the staircase.

A door slammed somewhere above them, and Marcy released her breath in a long, shuddering sigh. She turned to Paul. Now she could see the pain in his eyes as he stared into the distance.

"I don't care what she says. I won't give you custody," he said doggedly. "I promised Hillary. It's the only thing I can still do for my sister." His voice broke and he turned away as if loath to let her see his grief.

"There's no reason why you should cede custody," Marcy said, wanting to comfort him. "Certainly not on the basis of that outburst. Stephanie didn't mean it. She's simply trying to cope with her own pain and sense of loss. Unfortunately, at fifteen she doesn't have the emotional skills to do it. It's up to you to help her."

"How? By letting her do as she pleases?"

"No, of course not. You can help her by understanding where she's coming from. Adolescence is an awkward stage at best, and under these circumstances..." Marcy gestured vaguely.

"Yes, the circumstances . . ." Paul sounded unbearably tired. "But how could she have loved Hillary, yet be trying to replace her with you?" The question sounded as if it had been torn from him.

"It's because she loved Hillary so much that she's so desperate to replace her," Marcy explained. "Because of her loving relationship with your sister, Stephanie feels that a mother is absolutely essential to her happiness. Since your sister is beyond her reach, she's looking for a substitute. And her biological mother is certainly a reasonable choice."

She followed Paul into the living room, wanting at least to try to make him understand why Stephanie was so upset. She watched as he poured a generous splash of brandy into a squat crystal tumbler, took a long drink, then set the drink down and rubbed the back of his neck.

"You're the psychologist, so tell me. What was so wrong about asking that she finish her piano lesson? Those lessons were important to Hillary. It would only have meant a half-hour delay in meeting you, and if your flight had been delayed the way they usually are, not even that."

"I don't think the lesson is the real issue here. Not for her or for you."

"But—"

"I think you two are engaged in a power struggle."

"That's ridiculous. I'm the adult."

"That's undeniable, but what does that have to do with anything?"

"Adults make the rules."

"You can't possibly be that naive," Marcy said bluntly.

"I realize we're having a few adjustment problems."

"Rather on the scale of the San Andreas Fault," Marcy commented. "You, my friend, have an unenviable task. You are trying to guide a teenager through adolescence without having had the advantage of shared, happy memories and a deep, loving relationship to smooth the way. To make matters worse, you're both still reeling from a devastating emotional blow."

"The problems I already know," he said wryly. "It's the solutions I'm a little fuzzy on. Everything I read says that kids want and need firm limits."

"I think that comes under the heading of a little knowledge being a dangerous thing," she replied.

"Are you telling me that Stephanie doesn't want boundaries drawn?"

"No, I'm telling you that you need to decide which of your rules are going to be nonnegotiable and which aren't."

Paul frowned. "That's a contradiction in terms."

"No, it isn't. You need to decide which rules absolutely must be obeyed."

"You mean like her going to her music lessons, as Hillary wanted?"

"I was thinking more along the lines of not using drugs, not smoking—the kinds of things that are going to make a difference in her life ten years from now."

"It seems to me that if I give in on some things, she'll expect me to give in on everything," he said skeptically.

"On the contrary, I've found that if kids know there's some slack, they're more likely to cooperate on the hard-and-fast rules."

"Do you do much counseling?" he asked cautiously.

About to say yes, Marcy paused, suddenly aware that, except for the one afternoon a week when she volunteered two hours of her time to the local battered women's shelter, her private practice in the area she loved most had dwindled to almost nothing. Somehow, between teaching, research and trying to tie down the chair, counseling had fallen by the wayside.

"Does that silence mean that you're all theory and no practice?"

"Of course not." She saw no reason to go into detail. "I was simply thinking."

"You ought to be rethinking," he grumbled.

"Nonsense. Your method sure isn't working. Why not give mine a try? It doesn't pay to be rigid when dealing with kids."

"I am not rigid!" He looked down his nose at her, but when she merely raised her eyebrows gave her a sheepish smile.

"I will, however, admit to preferring my life to unfold along reasonably predictable lines. That's not the same thing as being rigid, though."

"It's not the same as being spontaneous, either."

"There is far too much spontaneity in the world."

"I didn't say impulsive, I said spontaneous. You ought to give it a shot sometimes. It—" The phone rang, and she broke off when Paul automatically reached for it.

He listened to a voice at the other end for a few minutes, then glanced once again at Marcy, his expression thoughtful.

"May I call you back in a few minutes, Dan?" he finally inquired. "I have a slight problem at this end."

A slight problem? Undoubtedly he meant her. To Paul she was "a slight problem" to be disposed of as quickly as possible, while to Bill Sidney she had been a well-padded model of rectitude who'd turned out to have feet of clay. She sighed. It seemed as though she needed to work on her image.

"Tired? I'll take you up to your room and you can rest before dinner."

His offer didn't fool her for a minute. Paul didn't care whether she was tired or not. He simply wanted her out of the way.

"That's quite all right. If you'll just point me in the right direction..." Marcy replied, planning to find Stephanie.

"Fine. Turn right at the top of the stairs. Your room is the third door on the left. I'll bring up your case in a bit."

Paul waited until she was out of earshot, then dialed the detective agency back. "You said you had the report ready on Marcy Handley?"

"Yup. Not that it took much effort on my part," Dan Fulton replied. "Her life's pretty much an open book. She graduated with honors from Stanford three years after your niece was born, earned a Ph.D. from Michigan in psychology and then joined the university in Indiana, where she's been ever since. She's well liked by her students, respected by her colleagues, and rumor has it that she's the front-runner for the chair of her department, which becomes vacant when the present head retires at the end of the year. And I checked out those documents in the adoption file. It really is her social security number and birth certificate. Your niece didn't confuse her with some other Marcy Handley."

"Hmm," Paul murmured, not really surprised by Fulton's report. Marcy exuded an intelligence and calm competence that tallied with those facts. The only thing that didn't tally was her continued refusal to admit that Stephanie was hers. That just made no sense. Not in light of the documents he had and the fact that she knew he had them. But in a weird way he rather liked her refusal to face the truth. Somehow it made her more human. She didn't have all the answers, either.

"Not only that," Fulton continued, "but recently she's gained quite a bit of public attention with a study she did last year on how a woman's clothing affects the way people see her. We found out she's signed with Doubleday to write a general-interest book, using the results. Rumor has it she got a very lucrative contract, but we couldn't pin down any numbers.

"She also teaches Sunday school at the Methodist church and volunteers one afternoon a week at the county's battered women's shelter," the detective concluded.

"She must have some vices," Paul said.

"If she does, she's keeping them well under wraps. I could dig a little deeper, if you like."

"No," Paul said after a moment's thought. "You've already covered what I really wanted to know. Thanks for the rush job. I appreciate it."

"Anytime, Mr. Wycoff."

Still thoughtful, Paul hung up, his gaze fixed on the pale cream wall in front of him, an image of Marcy's face in his mind's eye. Her eyes were sparkling with laughter, and her full lips were curved in a smile that invited him to share the joke. She seemed so full of life.

He felt an unsettling mixture of envy and longing. Marcy was like the sun coming out after a rainy day, and there hadn't been much sun in his life recently. Nonetheless, he knew it was a bad idea for him to get involved with her on any but the most superficial level. She represented a danger to what family he had left, as long as Stephanie saw in her a replacement for Hillary. But to his mind, if anyone was to replace Hillary in Stephanie's affections, he should be the one. After all, he was Hillary's brother and Stephanie's guardian, the one person willing to publicly claim her and their relationship. He'd been there for her after the accident. And he'd continue to be there for her, not Marcy, who would be returning to the university once this visit was over, and then what would happen? He certainly didn't intend to let Marcy take Stephanie back to Indiana. Stephanie was *his* concern. And it was probably better for Stephanie in the long run if Marcy continued to deny being her mother. Then again, maybe it wasn't.

3

MARCY PAUSED at the head of the stairs and listened, trying to figure out where Stephanie's room was. She didn't want to leave the girl so upset without at least having tried to talk to her.

A faint sound of music came from behind the second door on her left. She knocked gently. When there was no answer, she tried again.

"Go away." The muffled sound was Stephanie's voice.

"How far should I go? Back to Indiana?"

The door abruptly swung open. "I didn't know it was you, Marcy. I thought it was *him*."

Marcy smiled. "'Him' got a phone call. I thought I'd stop by and thank you for your welcome before I went to my room."

"Come in. Please." Stephanie stepped aside and gestured in invitation. "I'm sorry I yelled and caused a scene. Mom always said—" she swallowed hard "—that a good hostess never does anything to make a guest uncomfortable."

"That's okay." Marcy glanced curiously around, admiring the delicate Regency furniture, needlepoint carpet and sunny yellow wallpaper. It was a gorgeous room that bespoke both money and the knowledge of how to use it.

Stephanie must have noticed her interest. "It used to be my mom's room," she said. "Uncle Paul said she decorated it when she was in college."

"It's beautiful," Marcy said sincerely. She sat down on one of the love seats in front of the white marble fireplace. "Actually, I think my first apartment would have fit into this room with space left over."

"It's the second-biggest bedroom in the house. I was kinda surprised when Uncle Paul let me have it."

"Why?"

"Because he likes it," Stephanie declared. "And he doesn't like me."

"He doesn't?"

"No." Stephanie sniffed back tears. "He doesn't. He wishes I'd never come to live with him."

"That's true enough. After all, if you'd never come to live with him, that would mean your mother was still alive, and he obviously loved her very much."

"Then why doesn't he ever talk about her? He never says anything about her or Dad. Or much else, for that matter. He just lays down a lot of rules and goes to work and comes home and asks me how my day was. How does he think my days are? My parents are both dead, and I'm in a new school where I don't know anyone but Jessie and I miss them so much. It's just not fair!" She dissolved into heartbroken little sobs.

Marcy waited patiently until Stephanie had cried herself out, then said, "I agree entirely."

"Huh?" Stephanie rubbed her fingers across her swollen eyelids.

"That life's unfair."

Stephanie gulped. "Our minister said that it was God's will and it was un-Christian to question the accident or to complain."

"Your minister sounds like an insensitive jerk who would benefit greatly from a basic course in human relations," Marcy replied tartly.

"And Uncle Paul doesn't even seem to care."

"Why do you say that?" Marcy asked.

"I told you. He never talks about them."

"You know, Stephanie, in our society men aren't encouraged to show their feelings. They're supposed to be strong and emotionless in the face of pain. And when you add to that the fact that some people are naturally very reserved..." She shrugged. "Just because your uncle doesn't show his feelings, it doesn't mean he doesn't have any."

"I guess." Stephanie didn't sound too certain. "But why did it have to happen? Why? We were so happy."

Marcy sighed. "A lot of people ask that question but no one has come up with an answer yet. All you can do is try to cope with what happened."

"How?"

"By knowing that your feelings are normal. In time the pain will fade and happier memories will return."

"Will the...the emptiness ever go away?" Stephanie whispered.

"Not entirely," Marcy said honestly. "But I promise you that eventually it will become bearable. You'll be happy again. Not all at once, but in bits and pieces that will begin to string themselves together for longer and longer periods."

Stephanie looked up at her, then glanced down again. Finally she whispered, "How can I feel like that when they're dead?"

Marcy knew that wasn't simply a rhetorical question, so she waited.

"Yesterday, when my Latin teacher said that I'd done a great job on a translation, I felt so happy." Stephanie gulped back fresh tears. "For a few minutes I forgot all about what had happened and only thought about myself."

"Tell me, Stephanie, what kind of people were your parents?"

Stephanie sniffled. "Not perfect, really, but they were the best parents anyone could ask for."

"Do you think they would want you to be unhappy for the rest of your life because of what happened?"

"Of course not!" Stephanie looked shocked at the idea. "Mom always wanted everyone to be happy. That's why she kept trying to marry Uncle Paul off to one of her friends." She uttered a watery chuckle. "Dad always used to say that Uncle Paul would be a darn sight happier if she'd just let him wallow in his bachelor status."

Marcy smiled back. "My point is, Stephanie, that your parents wouldn't want you to be unhappy. What

I'd like you to do is to let yourself feel sad when you're sad, and when something happens that makes you happy, feel that, too."

Marcy got to her feet, figuring she'd given Stephanie enough to think about for the time being. "I'm going to unpack and rest for a while. It never ceases to amaze me how tired I get just sitting in a plane."

"I'll see you at dinner?" Stephanie asked eagerly.

"Without fail. I hate airline food, so I'm starved." Smiling again, Marcy left to find her own room.

Retracing her steps down the hallway, she paused in front of the third door on the left and knocked to be sure it was empty. When nothing happened, she stepped inside, whistling under her breath at the sight of yet more luxury. While not as big as Stephanie's room, this one was nonetheless easily four times the size of her bedroom at home. And furnished much more elegantly, from the antique Aubusson rug beneath her feet to the delicate Hepplewhite furniture.

Marcy kicked off her shoes and carefully draped the jacket of her tan suit over the back of one of the chaise longues in front of the fireplace.

She sank onto the bed, sighing pleasurably as she stretched out. She had been right to come. They really did need her help. Both Paul and Stephanie were so caught up in their own feelings that they hadn't given any thought to how the other one felt. Hopefully, she could at least get them talking to each other.

Tomorrow she'd ask to see those adoption papers. With luck there would be something either to confirm her suspicion that Pam was Stephanie's mother or, if not, to give her a clue as to who was.

Marcy frowned. If Stephanie were Pam's daughter, would that make her Marcy's second cousin or her first cousin once removed? She fell asleep before she could decide.

A BRISK RAP ON THE DOOR woke her. Marcy pried open her eyes and stared blankly at the unfamiliar surroundings. She heard a second knock.

"Marcy? Are you there?"

Paul! Recognition swept away the cloud of sleep still fogging her mind. She sat up and pushed her hair off her forehead.

"Just a second," she answered, swinging her legs over the edge of the bed and staggering to her feet.

"Aunt Clementia called. She asked me to bring you over for tea, since she can't come to dinner."

Marcy glanced at the clock on the wall over the bureau. Four-thirty. No wonder she felt so groggy. She couldn't have been asleep for more than half an hour.

"She lives in the cottage just behind the house," Paul coaxed.

"I'd love to meet her." Marcy stifled a yawn. "Just give me five minutes."

"I'll meet you down in the front hallway."

Marcy slipped her feet into her shoes and, looking for a bathroom, she opened one of the doors in the far wall. It was a closet. She was luckier on her second try. That door led to a large bathroom, decorated in functional white ceramic tile. The only bits of color were the thick, fluffy blue towels hanging beside the sink and the blue and green throw rug in front of the huge, claw-footed tub.

"Shades of the thirties!" Marcy chuckled. She splashed cold water onto her face and briefly debated going downstairs to retrieve her purse, which contained her makeup.

"To heck with it," she muttered. Considering the fact that he'd woken her from a nap, seeing her au naturel was as much as he had a right to expect.

As she passed Stephanie's room, she stopped and listened, but there was no longer any sound from inside. Pausing at the head of the stairs, she looked down. Paul was standing in front of the hall table, studying a sheet of yellow, legal-size paper. The afternoon sunlight pouring through the fanlight above the door drenched him in a golden haze, so that he seemed to glow with light.

"Ah, there you are." The very normalcy of his response dispelled the brief sense of unreality.

"Isn't Stephanie coming with us?" she asked when she got to the bottom of the stairs.

"No, she's in the basement looking for spiders."

Marcy stared at him. "She's where, doing what?"

"She said it's an extra credit project for her biology class." He grimaced. "I hope she doesn't find any. I can't abide large hairy things, and if there are any living in my house, I'd just as soon not know about it."

Marcy shuddered. "You and me both."

"We'll go out the back way. Aunt Clementia lives in a cottage at the rear of the property. It gives her a feeling of being independent, but she's still close enough that I can keep an eye on her."

"Exactly how old is she?" Marcy inquired, remembering Stephanie's comments.

"She'll be eighty next Thursday. I want to explain a little about my aunt," he went on slowly. "She's...she's just the slightest bit eccentric about some things."

"Oh?" Marcy studied his embarrassed expression with sudden interest. "What things?"

"Nothing serious," he assured her. "She says that at her age she's earned the right to please herself and never mind what anyone else thinks. She's an old maid, you know."

Marcy waited a few minutes for him to elaborate, and when he didn't she asked, "What's the connection?"

"I just meant that she never had a family to occupy her time. So she found other things. Like . . . the unexplained."

Marcy frowned. "Why can't you explain it?"

"No, I meant she's interested in the unexplained."

"You mean like ghosts and fortune-telling?"

"Unfortunately, yes. She's absolutely fascinated by the whole lot. And you are not to say anything snide," he ordered.

"If I say something snide, it won't be to a harmless little old lady, but to you," she snapped. "What have I ever done to make you think I'd make fun of her?"

"Oh, hell!" Paul shoved his fingers through his hair in a gesture of frustration. "I didn't mean that you ... It's just ... Sometimes people think it's a little strange...."

"*People* need more to fill their time. However, I will acquit you of a personal insult," she said magnanimously. "You were just putting your foot in your mouth in a general sort of way."

"I seem to be making a career of it lately. I was simply trying to protect my aunt. She's the dearest old soul, and it scares me that she's going to be eighty. Sometimes I feel as if I can almost see her fading away."

Marcy sighed. "I know exactly what you mean. My grandmother is in her nineties."

She stopped suddenly, staring in front of her in obvious delight. Her eyes gleamed with interest and her lips were parted in surprise, giving Paul an enticing view of the very tip of a pink tongue caught between even white teeth.

"What is that?" she demanded.

"What's what?" He looked to see what had caught her attention, but saw nothing out of the ordinary.

"All those flowers." She pointed to the eight-foot-wide carpet of blooms that ringed his aunt's small English-style cottage.

"Oh, those. That's her moat."

"Moat?" Marcy walked closer. "I thought moats had water and an occasional monster at the bottom."

"As well as mold, algae, mildew, damp basements, drowned pets and mosquitoes," he added.

Marcy sniffed disparagingly. "You, sir, have no romance in your soul. Think of it," she continued dreamily. "Your very own moat with a drawbridge you could raise to keep out the world."

"And do you want to keep the world at bay?" he asked curiously.

Marcy grimaced. "I'm the psychologist. I'm the one who's supposed to ask questions like that. At any rate, it's much too nice a day to go delving into anyone's psyche. What did you tell your aunt?"

"About what?" He followed her over the sturdy wooden bridge that spanned the flowers.

"About me!" she exclaimed in exasperation. "I want to know what lies you told her that I'm going to have to deny."

"I told her the truth," he said defensively. "I never lie."

"We all lie occasionally," she insisted. "Some of us are just a lot more honest about doing it."

"I only told her the truth," he insisted doggedly.

"Whose truth? Yours? Mine? Stephanie's? The truth means a lot of different things to a lot of different people, and so far I haven't heard your truth sound much like mine."

"Now that little diatribe sounds just as if it came from a psychologist," Paul snapped back, annoyed by her continued refusal to face facts.

"Why, you—"

"Ah, my dears, how good of you to come to tea."

Marcy spun around at the sound of the elderly woman's voice. A stick-thin woman with snow-white hair arranged in a wispy knot on the top of her head was smiling at them in delight. Her violet silk dress was swaying in the slight breeze, giving her an ethereal air that Marcy would have been willing to bet had been carefully thought out. There was far too much intelligence behind those faded blue eyes now studying her so intently. Clementia might be eccentric, but Marcy was certain that she was no one's fool.

"So you're Stephanie's mother," Clementia said. "I can't begin to tell you what a blessing your daughter has been to us."

"I'm sure she is. Unfortunately, I'm not responsible, because I am not Stephanie's mother," Marcy said firmly, beginning to feel that she should have a recording made.

"Oh?" Clementia glanced uncertainly at Paul. "I must have misunderstood. Well, no matter. Come in and have tea, anyway."

Clementia's small house smelled of lilacs, ginger cookies and bygone dreams. The aromas tugged at elusive memories from Marcy's childhood, making her feel safe and protected, secure from the cares of the world.

The sitting room was a soothing blend of English country style and Chippendale antiques. Marcy sat down on a yellow chintz sofa that felt as if it was stuffed with goose down, sinking into the thick cushions. When Paul sat beside her, his weight tipped her toward him, and she dug her toes into the needlepoint carpet to hold herself steady. She refused to give in to the temptation to allow herself to sag against him. She was already too close for comfort. Not only was the wool of his suit jacket brushing against her arm, but she could smell the faint aroma of the cologne he was wearing. It was like the tang of the sea in the early-morning sun.

Trying to concentrate on something else, she focused on the coffee table in front of her. On its highly polished mahogany surface stood a collection of knickknacks, but the place of honor was reserved for a truly magnificent glass ball that sat on an intricately worked silver pedestal.

Marcy leaned closer, fascinated by the way the light streaming through the French doors behind them was creating a rainbow deep within the ball.

"Would you like cream and sugar or lemon in your tea, Miss Handley?" Clementia asked.

"Lemon, please." Marcy absently accepted a cup, her attention still on the ball. "This is a magnificent piece," she said.

"Isn't it, though?" Clementia beamed at her. "Paul brought it back from a trip to India last year. The poor dear had to lug it around for two weeks through three different countries."

"Did he?" Marcy glanced at him and saw him shrug. It would seem that while he didn't approve of his aunt's exotic hobbies, he was still willing to indulge her.

"Are you interested in reading the future, Miss Handley?" Clementia asked eagerly.

"Just Marcy, please, and yes, I am."

"You are?" Paul asked suspiciously.

"Certainly. I'd love to be able to see into the future. Into other people's futures, at least."

Clementia smiled at her approvingly. "And just think of being able to contact the spirit world."

Paul frowned at Marcy. "I didn't mean you should encourage her," he said in an undertone.

"Why not?" Marcy whispered back. "You do."

"Yes, why not?" Clementia eyed him over the top of her glasses. "I may be getting old, young man, but all my parts still work, including my ears."

"It's one thing to dabble in the unexplained, but everyone knows that there is no such thing as a spirit." Paul reeled off the words as if he'd had lots of practice.

"Speak for yourself," Marcy said.

"He's a nonbeliever, you know." Clementia shook her head sadly. "He just refuses to keep an open mind."

"Predicting the future is impossible," Paul declared.

"Not necessarily," Marcy said seriously. "A California university did a very famous study some years back, in which they had people try to predict which cards would come up in a random sequence. Interestingly enough, some people were consistently able to predict the right card at a far greater rate than could be explained by chance."

"You can't possible believe that they were psychic?" Paul stared at her earnest expression in dismay. He hadn't wanted to make his aunt feel uncomfortable, but certainly hadn't intended that Marcy should aid and abet her. With Marcy's vitality to add impetus to Clementia's stubborn beliefs . . . He shuddered to think of what might happen.

"Let's just say that I don't disbelieve it," Marcy said slowly. "There are far too many things in this world that can't be explained logically for me to ever dismiss any idea out of hand."

"You're serious, aren't you?" he said uneasily.

Marcy smiled at him. "Right in one."

"It was so good of you to bring Marcy by to tea, my dear." Clementia beamed at him. "But I know how busy you are. Don't feel obligated to stay."

Paul chuckled. "Was that a tactful way of telling me to get lost, so that you two can plot who knows what without my interjecting reason into your schemes?"

"You don't have to go far," Clementia coaxed. "I just want to talk to Marcy alone for a few minutes. Why don't you pull a few weeds out of the flowers in the moat?"

"Five minutes?" He didn't want Clementia to tire herself out. This was her evening for the ladies' altar society, and he knew she'd insist on going, no matter what.

"Five minutes," Clementia agreed.

When he'd left, she leaned closer to Marcy. "Now we can have a comfortable coze. Tell me. If you aren't Stephanie's mother, why did you come?"

Her directness startled Marcy. "To try to find out who is," she said.

"Mmm." Clementia studied Marcy for a long moment. "You won't listen, because the young never do, but I'll tell you, anyway. Let sleeping dogs lie."

"But this sleeping dog is wearing a collar with my name on it, and I want to know why.

"For instance, do you remember if Hillary ever said anything about Stephanie's birth mother? Anything at all, no matter how insignificant?"

Clementia stared blankly past Marcy, as if looking down the long corridor of years. "I never met Stephanie's birth mother. I understood she lived in an apartment somewhere in Chicago before the baby was born. Hillary used to visit her there. Oh, there was one thing. When Stephanie's hair finally started to come in, Hillary said that it was a shame that she hadn't inherited her mother's red highlights."

Marcy found herself touching her own short hair, inexplicably feeling guilty because it had gleaming red highlights.

Pam had the same hair coloring, and so did most of her cousins. But if Stephanie's birth mother had gone to the trouble of stealing her identification, it was quite possible that she'd also decided to use a color rinse in order to perfect her impersonation. Marcy decided to keep probing.

"Hillary didn't mention anything else? There were no pictures or anything like that?"

Clementia shook her head. "Not that I ever saw. Hillary didn't want constant reminders around that Stephanie was adopted." She paused a moment, then said, "Please try to make sure that Stephanie doesn't get hurt by all this. She's going through a very rough patch at the moment. I try to help her, but I'm not as young as I used to be."

"I'll be careful," Marcy promised. The last thing she wanted was to hurt either a defenseless adolescent already reeling under a series of body blows or this oddly appealing little old lady who was watching her out of the corner of her eye.

"Tell me," Clementia wanted to know, "what do you think of my nephew?"

Marcy took refuge in a platitude. "He seems rather nice."

"Hmm." Clementia pursed her lips, then said, "Finish your tea and I'll tell your fortune."

Seeing no harm in humoring her, Marcy drained her cup, handed it to Clementia and leaned forward.

Clementia peered into the cup, carefully studying the pattern of the tea leaves on the bottom. Finally she raised her head and stared worriedly at Marcy over the rim of her bifocals.

Marcy felt a shiver of unease at Clementia's sober expression. "If it's bad news, please don't tell me."

"It's not *your* bad news," Clementia said slowly. "But there's a dark stain of evil spreading out to touch you." Her fingers began to tremble and she hurriedly set the cup down.

"Aunt Clementia!" Marcy grasped the frail, chilled fingers in her own, much warmer ones. "Are you all right?"

"Certainly, dear. I've probably got it wrong, anyway." She gave Marcy a wobbly smile. "No method of predicting the future is ever entirely accurate."

"Not true," Marcy replied, trying to lighten the curiously oppressive atmosphere. "I can guarantee that if you don't rest, Paul will have my head for upsetting you."

"I'm not precisely upset," Clementia assured her. "Just a little surprised. It never ceases to amaze me what interesting curves life occasionally throws at us."

Marcy eyed her uncertainly. She still didn't know precisely what this was all about, but she wasn't willing to run the risk of further upsetting Clementia. Forcing a smile, she got to her feet.

"I've already used up five minutes and then some. I'll stop by to see you again, if I may."

"I'll look forward to it, dear." Clementia gave her a singularly sweet smile.

Marcy sighed deeply as she left the cottage. No one could say that she wasn't finding plenty to occupy her mind. She looked around, wondering what had happened to Paul. Had he returned to the house instead of waiting for her? She rounded the corner of the cottage and suddenly saw him.

He was standing, literally knee deep in orange marigolds, in the middle of the flower moat with his back to her. He had taken off his suit jacket, hung it over the railing of the bridge and rolled up the sleeves of his white shirt. He was indeed pulling weeds.

She walked to the edge of the moat, the sound of her footsteps swallowed up by the lush grass. She was about to say something when Paul flung a handful of debris behind him, showering her with flying weeds and small clumps of dirt. Marcy let out a small yelp of surprise.

Paul swung around at the sound and stared at her. His firm lips quivered as he attempted to restrain his laughter.

"Sorry." He climbed out of the moat. "I guess I should have yelled 'fore!'"

"Yelling 'behind!' would have been more to the point."

"I said I was sorry." He pulled a piece of quack grass out of her hair. "You aren't going to turn out to be one of those people who hold grudges, are you?"

"Nope. I don't believe in holding grudges. It's unhealthy. I believe in getting even."

He shot her a suddenly wary glance. "Even?"

"Uh-huh. It's very cathartic."

"Okay. I'm truly sorry. Abjectly sorry. Let me make amends." He began to brush the tiny bits of dirt off the front of her pale yellow sweater.

Marcy's body immediately began to react to the touch of his hard fingers. Mesmerized, she glanced up. Paul's features seemed somehow sharper, his cheeks leaner, the bones of his face more prominent. She lifted her gaze slightly and felt as if she were falling into the depths of his liquid black eyes.

Now her gaze drifted lower, to focus on the line of his lips. She wanted to feel those lips against hers, she realized with a sense of shock. To explore their texture, their taste.

As if her desire had somehow communicated itself to him, he leaned forward and lightly, delicately, brushed his mouth against hers, sending a series of shivers chasing over her skin. Feeling her reaction, he flicked out his tongue to stroke her full bottom lip.

At that Marcy grasped his shoulders, feeling the crisp, sun-warmed cotton of his shirt beneath her fingertips as she sought the hard muscles beneath. The pungent aroma of marigolds and the more elusive scent of the soil teased her nostrils, adding something elemental to the kiss.

Much too soon for her intoxicated senses, Paul raised his head and gave her a long, thoughtful look.

"What was that in aid of?" she asked.

"My mother always used to say, 'Kiss and make it better.'" He brushed the dirt off his hands and picked up his jacket.

Maybe, she thought, but in her experience, "it" didn't get any better than that.

4

THE CLOCK IN HER BEDROOM gave a funny little clink as it marked the hour. Marcy checked the time against her wristwatch, closed the bureau on the last of her unpacking and then checked herself one last time in the gilt mirror over the mantel. She turned slightly to look at the back of her jade silk shirtwaist and, satisfied, left her bedroom.

Paul had said that dinner was served at seven and she didn't want to be late. Not only would it be impolite, but she was starving. She followed the delicious aroma of dinner down the stairs to the dining room. Pausing on the threshold, she peered in.

A Queen Anne table that looked big enough to seat twenty stood in the center of the room. Above it, a truly magnificent chandelier sprayed droplets of fragmented light upon the two people below. Paul sat at the head of the table, fixedly staring into his wineglass. On his left, with her back to the door, sat Stephanie, who seemed fascinated by the arrangement of her silverware. The silence was oppressive.

Marcy frowned thoughtfully. Those two needed something to make them pull together. But what? The tragedy certainly hadn't done it. Perhaps they needed something they both felt strongly about; something that didn't threaten their happiness.

Paul looked up and saw her. "Come in," he said and got to his feet.

"Thank you." Marcy slipped into the chair he held for her. "It smells delicious down here."

"Mrs. Bailey is a great cook," Stephanie said, showing some animation. "Especially chocolate-chip cookies."

"Mrs. Bailey is my housekeeper," Paul explained. "She prepares a meal for us in the evening before she leaves."

"I met your Aunt Clementia while you were hunting spiders, Stephanie," Marcy said, venturing what she hoped was a safe conversational gambit. "She's a darling."

"Yes, isn't she?" Stephanie's eyes brightened. "Did she read your tea leaves?"

"Sort of. I was disappointed. I was expecting visions of a future full of wealth and tall, dark strangers," Marcy told her, trying to suppress the disquiet she'd felt at Clementia's unexpected reading.

"Nah," Stephanie scoffed. "Aunt Clementia says that kind of fortune-telling is strictly for amateurs."

"You can't tell the future," Paul muttered into his wine.

"Yes, you can," Stephanie retorted. "Don't you think so, Marcy?"

Marcy decided there was no time like the present to try to teach them how to communicate with each other.

"I think that whoever said that you should never, ever argue politics, religion or the supernatural with anyone was right."

"Never?" Stephanie asked incredulously.

"Never!" Marcy repeated emphatically. "And for an excellent reason. People's opinions on those subjects tend to be based on feelings, not on reason. Your best bet is to simply state your case, listen politely to the other person's point of view, no matter how idiotic it might sound, then change the subject.

"Why don't you give it a try, Stephanie? Tell your uncle how you feel about the supernatural."

Stephanie grimaced. "Why? He already knows how I feel."

Marcy nodded. "True, but you can practice on him, anyway. Go on. Give it a shot."

Stephanie heaved a put-upon sigh and said, "If that's what you want. Uncle Paul, I believe that sometimes, in the right circumstances, some people can foretell the future."

"And I think that's a load of—"

Marcy cleared her throat.

"Garbage," he finished.

Both speakers looked inquiringly at Marcy.

"Now we change the subject," she said. "Let's try an old tried-and-true standby. How was school today?"

"Pretty good," Stephanie said. "I found six huge spiders down in the basement, over where Aunt Clementia said the old root cellar used to be when she was little. I'll bet nobody else finds anywhere near that many, so

I'm sure to get an A. And you'll never guess what happened during Latin class."

"Your Latin teacher had an attack of Roman culture and sold the principal to a traveling circus?" Marcy suggested with a straight face.

Stephanie giggled. "Don't we just wish."

"Somebody put Out of Order signs on all the teachers' rest rooms?" Paul inquired.

"We don't do such juvenile things," Stephanie said loftily. "Besides, teachers have a nasty way of getting even," she added.

"So tell us what happened," Marcy urged.

"I was invited to help with the decorating for the Harvest Moon Dance on Saturday," Stephanie said, her pleasure almost visible.

"Congratulations," Marcy said encouragingly. "What kind of theme are you using?"

"Oh, just things that get harvested. You know, like pumpkins and corn shocks and that kind of stuff. Evan, the senior who's in charge of everything, says his grandfather has a farm and we can have whatever we want. Jessie's mom'll be by to pick me up after dinner. She's giving a bunch of us a ride. A couple of the upperclassmen are driving pickup trucks, and we're going out to the farm tonight to get all the stuff we need. We're going to do the actual decorating tomorrow night." Marcy saw her shoot Paul a wary glance.

Paul frowned. "On a school night?"

"It has to be then," Stephanie insisted. "There won't be time to get the stuff and set it up tonight. Friday night we're playing a football game, and Saturday is the dance. So that only leaves tomorrow."

Paul frowned. "All right, but make sure you're home by nine-thirty both nights."

"Nine-thirty!" Stephanie gasped. "Nobody else will have to leave then. Everyone will think I'm a baby!"

"Everyone will think you have someone who cares about your getting a proper amount of rest," Paul countered.

Stephanie jumped to her feet, visibly angry. "You don't understand. You just—"

Marcy, who had been listening silently so far, put her fingers into her mouth and emitted a piercing whistle. It stopped Stephanie in midtirade. Both she and Paul jerked around and stared in surprise.

"Please sit down, Stephanie." Marcy waited until she complied, then continued. "I think the two of you could use a referee, but only if you both agree."

"A referee?" Stephanie eyed her suspiciously.

"I think she means something like binding arbitration," Paul said.

"No, I mean something like a moderator in a rational discussion," Marcy corrected him.

"We were having a rational discussion," Paul insisted.

"That isn't what it sounded like to me. Now, do we give my method a try, or do I take my dinner into the kitchen and let you two spoil each other's appetites?"

"But—" Paul began.

"Yes or no," Marcy interjected. "Just think, the ulcer you prevent may be your own."

Paul shrugged. "All right, yes."

Marcy turned to the girl. "Stephanie?"

"I guess," she muttered.

Marcy shook her head. "No guesses. Yes or no. You choose."

"Yes." Stephanie heaved a long-suffering sigh. "Now what?"

"Now I state the situation as I understand it. Then each of you may correct anything you feel I've gotten wrong."

"Okay." Stephanie nodded, beginning to look intrigued.

"As I understand it, Stephanie has a school-night curfew of nine-thirty and wishes an exception tonight and tomorrow night, so that she can participate in a special event. Is that right?" She looked at Stephanie, who nodded.

"Yes, but she needs her rest," Paul pointed out.

"True," Marcy agreed, "but we aren't discussing doing away with the curfew. We're discussing lifting it for two nights."

"Actually only one night," Stephanie said. "They said that tonight it would only take an hour and a half or so. It's only tomorrow night when we do the decorating that I'll be late."

"You'll be tired in the morning," Paul said.

"Let's try the worst-case scenario," Marcy suggested. "What's the worst thing that can happen if you stay out late on a school night and don't get enough sleep, Stephanie?"

"I'll be tired Friday, like Uncle Paul said. But I don't have any tests scheduled, and I can sleep late on Saturday morning."

"Maybe," Paul conceded.

"Now, Stephanie," Marcy went on. "You explain to your uncle why you think he should make an exception to the rule tomorrow night."

"Well . . ." Stephanie pushed her food around on her plate with her fork for a moment, then said, "Because I like some of the kids who are doing the decorating. I think they could be my friends. The only friend I've made so far at this school is Jessie, and lots of times she's busy with other things."

"I suppose friends *are* worth the loss of a little sleep," Paul said slowly.

Stephanie frowned at him. "Does that mean yes?"

"Yes, but make sure you're home by—"

"Eleven," she inserted hurriedly. "They lock the gym at ten forty-five."

"All right, eleven," Paul conceded.

Stephanie gave him a relieved smile and jumped to her feet. "Thanks. I'm going to go phone Jessie and tell her I can go."

"But your dinner," Paul called after her.

"I'll eat there. There'll be donuts and soda." She disappeared into the kitchen.

"Very well done," Marcy said seriously.

"I didn't know she didn't have friends," he said. "And I should have. This is a new school, and it's much bigger than the one she used to go to."

"It takes time to make friends."

"I wonder what kind of kids they are?" Paul mused.

Marcy laughed. "Has anyone ever told you that you're a born worrier?"

He grimaced. "I never used to be." He swallowed the lump in his throat and forced himself to continue. "Before Hillary died, all I ever worried about was the stock market, the state of the world economy and what Aunt Clementia was getting up to when my back was turned. Now that I have Stephanie, I'm finding out that there's nothing like a teenager to add depth and scope to one's worrying."

"You'll both do fine once you get past the shakedown period."

Paul chuckled unexpectedly. "You make us sound like the maiden voyage of a battleship."

She smiled back at him. "A nuclear-powered one when you're dealing with a teenager."

"Now that Stephanie's evening is taken care of, what are *we* going to do?" he asked.

Marcy felt a flash of intense pleasure and ruthlessly jettisoned her plan to begin to organize the notes for her book. She could work on them all day tomorrow while Paul was at the office and Stephanie was at school, she told herself firmly.

"What are my choices?" she asked.

"Well, I don't want to leave the house in case..." His gaze strayed to where Stephanie had been sitting.

"Fine with me," she said cheerfully, understanding his fears. "There's a special on PBS later tonight on the emerging economies of the former Soviet Union that sounds interesting."

"It does?" She saw Paul eye her with sudden interest.

"Uh-huh. Not the economy so much as its effects on the people."

"I'll watch it with you. I'm curious as to what they have to say. Eastern Europe is a real economic growth area right now. I just want to walk down and visit with Aunt Clementia for a few minutes first, to make sure she's well enough to go to her church meeting."

Paul really was a very caring man, Marcy reflected. He just didn't always know quite how to express that concern in a positive way.

"While you do that, I'll call my mother and let her know I arrived without running into muggers or an airline disaster," she said.

"Feel free to use my study," he offered.

"Thank you." Marcy picked up her fork and finally began to eat. Maybe she'd get lucky, she thought hopefully. Maybe her mother would have something to report about Pam.

But despite trying before, during and after the PBS special, Marcy wasn't able to reach her mother. Finally she left a message on her parents' answering machine, telling them that she'd arrived safely and would call the following afternoon.

HER MOTHER ANSWERED on the second ring.

"Hi, Mom, it's me."

"Hello, darling. How's Boston?"

"Boston's fine, but I can't say the same for my investigative powers. I wasn't able to discover anything in that adoption file that I didn't already know. There's nothing even remotely personal in it. Just the bare legal documents. Although coming here hasn't been a total waste of time," Marcy said slowly. An image of Paul's animated features as he'd explained the implications of free trade on the economy at dinner last night floated through her mind.

"I had better luck. I tell you, Marcy, I missed my calling. I should have been another Miss Marple."

Marcy chuckled. "Might I remind you that Miss Marple's specialty was discovering bodies."

"Skeletons in the family closet are enough for me, thank you. Your cousin, Pam, came to see me this morning."

"She did? Did you find out anything?"

"Yes. I don't think Pam is Stephanie's mother. In fact, if I were a betting woman, I'd put money on it."

"Why did she come to see you?"

"She said she tried to call you at the university yesterday and couldn't reach you. She wanted me to tell you that you could count on her support, and if there was anything she could do to make the process of easing Stephanie into the family any simpler, to let her know."

Marcy frowned at the picture over the mantel. "Why did that make you think she isn't Stephanie's mother?"

"It didn't. What convinced me was her pep talk to me about everyone doing impulsive things when they were young and too inexperienced to realize what the consequences might be. She told me that I should be grateful all you did was get pregnant. She said that while you were having Stephanie, she was going through her Joan of Arc period. She said she renounced the materialistic world, quit school, joined an activist group, and went to South America to save the world."

"I vaguely remember Pam lecturing me once about the poor and oppressed, but to be honest, I didn't pay a great deal of attention to her. What happened?"

"She said she discovered that the world didn't want to be saved. At least the part of it that governments control. She spent eight months in jail for urging a group of underpaid workers to form a union. The organization she was working for finally got her released, on condition she leave the country immediately."

"Yes, I can picture Pam leading an insurrection," Marcy said. "I see what you mean, though. If she was out of the country, she could hardly be Stephanie's mother. But why didn't the family know anything about it at the time?"

"Because Pam's mother is a numbskull!" Mrs. Handley declared. "Pam said she was so horrified at having a daughter in jail that she never said a word to anyone and begged Pam not to. Pam said she herself felt bad enough about all the trouble and expense she'd already caused her parents, so she kept quiet."

"Honestly!" Marcy snorted in disgust. "How my idiot aunt can equate being put in jail for trying to help the oppressed with serving a jail term . . . But be that as it may, it means I've lost my leading candidate for the position of Stephanie's mother."

"And I've a good mind to strike her mother off my Christmas card list."

Something suddenly clicked in Marcy's mind. "What did you say?"

"What?"

"About Christmas cards," Marcy said excitedly. "You send Christmas cards."

"It's a little late to get excited about it, dear. I've been doing it for forty years."

"Yes, but people send them back to you."

"That's the way it usually works," Mrs. Handley agreed.

"Signed."

"Of course, but . . . Oh," Mrs. Handley said slowly.

"Precisely. If Stephanie's mother really is a member of our family, it's more than likely she sends you Christmas cards. If we were to compare the signatures on your old cards with the signature on the release of custody form . . . You do save the cards, don't you?" Marcy asked anxiously.

"From one year to the next I do. That way I can tell who I owe them to. Do you know how to compare signatures, dear?"

"No, but I know someone at the university who does. Mom, have you got a pencil?"

"Just a minute, dear, while I . . . Ah, there. I found one. Go on."

"Send the cards to Daniel Santiago at the university's Criminology Department. I'll call him later and explain to him what I need."

"I'll make sure I include a signature from everyone in the family, if I have to go through all the old boxes in the attic and find letters. Although, you know, Marcy, it occurred to me after talking to Pam that it takes two to have a baby."

"No!" Marcy said in mock wonder. "Nobody can say my mother is slow on the uptake."

"I'm serious, Marcy. What if Stephanie's link to our family is through one of your *male* cousins? One of their girlfriends could have gotten pregnant, and they could have borrowed your records as easily as any of your female cousins."

"Damn!" The truth of what her mother was saying sank in. "That's just what this situation needed. Another curve."

"I'm sorry, dear, but I really felt I should mention it."

"Let's see." Marcy mentally sifted through her male cousins. "David would have been only twelve. That's too young. But that still leaves Martin, Ed, Jim and Ryan."

"Yes, but remember that Martin was going with the oldest Ekton girl. The one who married the optometrist and moved to Omaha. Martin was nuts about her, so he wouldn't have cheated on her, and she was at all the family gatherings that year. There's no way she could have been pregnant and kept it a secret."

"So we can eliminate Martin."

"Jim, too. That was the year the poor boy had so much trouble with acne. He was so self-conscious about his looks that he never even invited a girl to his junior prom. I doubt that he'd have been sleeping with anyone."

"Which leaves Ed and Ryan. I think I'll put them at the bottom of my list of suspects, because it's a lot harder to trace a baby through its father," Marcy said slowly. "Were you able to get in touch with Grandmother?"

"Yes, and let me tell you, it's not easy trying to get information from someone without coming right out and asking. Especially not from someone as sharp as your grandmother."

Marcy chuckled. "I can imagine. Did you find out anything?"

"Not specifically, but there was something in her tone of voice when she was talking about that general time period...." Mrs. Handley paused as if trying to clarify her thoughts. "I thought at first it was because that was the year your grandfather died, but I think it's more than that. I may be imagining things, but I think she knows something. Something she'd rather not."

"Interesting," Marcy said. "If you should find out anything else, would you let me know?"

"Certainly. Will you still be there in Boston? Or will you be leaving shortly?"

Leaving? Her mother's question caught Marcy off guard and she frowned again at the painting. An image of Paul superimposed itself upon the portrait. His dark eyes were narrowed to gleaming slits, and his lips were lifted in laughter. An answering warmth twisted through her stomach.

"Marcy, are you still there?"

"Mmm, sorry. I was thinking." Marcy forced her thoughts back to the present. "Yes, I'm going to be here a little while longer. Thanks for the help, Mom."

"Anytime. Take care, dear, and call if you need anything."

"I will. Love you." Marcy hung up and began to consider her mother's words. She'd managed to eliminate one suspect, only to add two more. At this rate she'd never find out who Stephanie's mother was. Being a detective was not as easy as it appeared on television.

"Mmm, Dr. Handley?" The housekeeper stuck her head around the study door.

"Yes?" The woman came into the room and Marcy got a good look at her face. She looked positively green. "Are you all right, Mrs. Bailey?"

"No, ma'am," she said simply. "I feel sick. If it's all right with you, I'm going home. I called my daughter and she's here now."

"Of course it's all right with me. I'll explain to Mr. Wycoff tonight."

"Tell him I'm sorry. And I haven't even started dinner yet," Mrs. Bailey said sadly.

"Not to worry," Marcy soothed. "I'll take care of everything. You just go home and get into bed.'

Mrs. Bailey swallowed uneasily. "There's a sirloin tip roast in the refrigerator for this evening that'll need to be put in the oven at three. And the baking potatoes are on the counter."

"Don't worry, Mrs. Bailey," Marcy repeated. "I'll see they don't starve. You go home and stay there until you're entirely well again."

"Don't worry, Dr. Handley. The way I feel at the moment, I couldn't do anything else."

Marcy picked up a pencil and began to plan the rest of her afternoon. She needed to call Daniel to tell him to expect the Christmas cards. Then she should call several key members of the Psychology Department to make sure they weren't wavering in their support. She tapped the pencil's eraser against her teeth in exasperation. It was all simply too Victorian for words. Even if Stephanie were her daughter, it should have no effect on her candidacy for the chair. Her own competence and experience, and the ideas she had for the future direction of the department were the things that should matter.

Marcy sighed. Perhaps she should just start with a short call to each of them, ostensibly to talk about department business. Then she could turn the conversation to Stephanie. It would be tricky trying to defend herself without running the risk of protesting too much, but at least she had to try, she decided. She'd worked too hard and too long for this opportunity to let it go down the tubes without a struggle. She added the names of four more colleagues to her list of people to call.

After that, she'd continue her work on the notes for her book. It was turning out to be a far more time-consuming job than she'd expected.

That left dinner to prepare. She nibbled on the eraser, remembering her thought last night that Paul and Stephanie needed something threatening to pull them together. What could be more threatening to a pair who seemed to thrive on red meat, high-cholesterol dishes, soda and donuts than a healthy, vegetarian meal? A wicked smile curved her lips.

Marcy tossed her pencil onto the pad and got to her feet. She'd take a break from her work and go to the grocery store. She could hardly wait to see the expression on their faces when she served dinner.

"POOR MRS. BAILEY," Stephanie lamented, staring suspiciously at her alfalfa, bean sprout and mushroom salad.

"You shouldn't have bothered, Marcy," Paul said with absolute sincerity. "We could have eaten out."

"I like to cook," Marcy said with what she hoped was an innocent smile. "It was a nice break from my work."

"Mmm, Marcy..." Stephanie poked one of the small white cubes that sat on her plate, covered with a thick tomato sauce. "What is this?"

"Tofu cacciatore," Marcy said, ignoring Paul's expression. "It's a marvelous source of easily digestible, low-cholesterol protein."

"But what is it?" Stephanie persisted.

"Soybean curds." Marcy was hard-pressed not to laugh as Paul and Stephanie exchanged looks of horror.

"Mrs. Bailey said we were going to have sirloin tip roast and baked potatoes with butter and sour cream and fresh asparagus with hollandaise sauce and hot apple pie with extrasharp cheddar cheese," Paul said plaintively.

"And a cholesterol level of over four hundred to go with it, no doubt," Marcy pointed out.

"I'll have you know that my cholesterol count is under two hundred." Now Paul was on the defensive.

"Even so, at your age you should be watching what you eat."

"My age!" Paul repeated as defense gave way to outrage.

Stephanie unexpectedly came to his aid. "He isn't all that old. He's got lots of good years left."

"At least six or seven," Marcy agreed. "But if he changes his ways and eats his veggies and tofu, he might stretch it to eight or nine."

The grandfather clock in the hall struck seven.

"Good heavens, is it that late already?" Stephanie exclaimed. "I'd really like to stay and try your—" she stared at her plate "—stuff. But I promised I'd be at the gym a little early to get started on the decorations."

"I'll take you." Paul jumped up with remarkable alacrity. He'd take her, all right. To the nearest McDonald's, unless Marcy missed her guess.

"You don't mind, do you, Marcy?" Stephanie asked.

"No, not at all," Marcy said sincerely. She would have preferred that they at least taste her tofu creation, but her little tactic had worked. "I can always reheat the tofu tomorrow."

She started to eat her own dinner with gusto. After the meal she'd try to reach Daniel again, something she had been trying to do all afternoon.

SHE FINALLY MANAGED to reach him at his home. "Daniel, this is Marcy Handley. I was beginning to think that I'd be reduced to leaving a message on the answering machine in your office."

"That's what it's for," Daniel said mildly.

"It's too public. I don't want this blabbed all over the campus until I have my facts straight. There are already enough rumors going around."

"I'll say," Daniel agreed wholeheartedly. "I as good as called Elliot Fielding over in administration a liar when he claimed an unimpeachable source had told him that you had a teenage daughter you'd kept hidden away and were now trying to disown."

"Oh, my God!" Marcy groaned. "I don't believe this!"

"Believe it. Joe Abernathy is feeding the rumors for all he's worth, in the hope that he'll get the chair instead of you. And that wimp Sidney is helping him."

"How could anyone who knows anything about me even listen to such a wild story, let alone repeat it?"

"You're the psychologist. You tell me. What can I do for you besides defend what's left of your good name?"

"I want you to compare all of the signatures on the Christmas cards my mother is sending you with the signature on the document I'm mailing and see if any of them match."

He chuckled. "In addition to all your other troubles, someone is forging your name on Christmas cards?"

"No. Someone forged my name on a child's birth certificate."

"Oh, so that's what happened. Interesting."

"'Interesting' is not quite the way I would have put it," Marcy said glumly. "It's bad enough when your own mistakes come back to haunt you, but it's absolutely intolerable when someone else's do. Can you do it?"

"Provided the signatures are clear and complete, it should be child's play. Where can I reach you with the results?"

Marcy gave him Paul's number. "When do you think you can get to it?"

"I'm leaving for a five-day workshop on DNA testing in criminal investigation tomorrow, so it'll probably be a week or so. Is that going to be a problem?"

Marcy swallowed her impatience. She wanted this mess settled as soon as possible, but didn't know anyone else with Daniel's expertise and reputation who would do the comparison for her. And trying to find someone else would undoubtedly take longer than five days.

"A week'll be fine, Daniel. I really appreciate your help."

"Glad to be of assistance."

"Take care." Marcy hung up the phone and stared blankly out the window of Paul's study. There really wasn't much more she could do to solve the mystery and clear her way to the chair than she was already doing. Maybe she ought to concentrate on Stephanie and Paul's problems for the time being. A reluctant smile curved her lips as she remembered their disorderly retreat from the dinner table. She wished she could have gone with them, but that would have defeated her purpose—to bring them together.

5

HIGH HEELS ADD HEIGHT, and height adds to a woman's authority. Marcy's eyes strayed from her notes to Paul, who was sitting across from her, reading notes of his own. He certainly had an air of authority, yet he wasn't all that tall. Probably no more than five-eleven. Six feet, tops. But it wasn't just a matter of height, Marcy finally decided. It was his personality—the aura of barely leashed energy that seemed to surround him.

At that moment the energy seemed to be in distinct danger of slipping its leash. His long fingers tapped impatiently on the mahogany lamp table beside his chair in a rhythm that seemed to increase from one minute to the next. He glanced yet again at the clock, and Marcy's eyes followed. Ten-thirty. Stephanie wasn't due back from her decorating for another half hour. At this rate Paul would be a nervous wreck by the time she finally did get home.

He needed something to take his mind off the time. But what? Something to drain all that energy. Something like a quick jog around the block, fifty push-ups, or... Marcy licked her lower lip. Perhaps a kiss? Warmth feathered over her skin as she remembered the pressure of his lips, remembered their taste and texture. Kissing him might relieve some of that pent-up tension. Then again, it might not. Kissing him as she wanted to do might just add to the tension.

Paul's third frown at his watch in sixty seconds convinced her to quit thinking about the problem and do something.

"Want to play a game?" she asked.

"A game?" His dark eyes gleamed with sudden interest.

Marcy ignored the twist of tension that tightened around her chest and continued. "As in checkers or cards. Something to pass the time."

Paul grimaced. "It'd take a miracle to do that. I have never had an evening go by this slowly. Maybe I should run over to the school and wait for her?"

"Maybe you should think again," Marcy said. "If you show up there without an excellent reason, Stephanie's going to think you're checking up on her."

He sighed. "I know that in my head. It's my heart that's having problems. This parenting business is a lot harder on the nerves than it looks from the outside."

"It'll get easier with practice," Marcy assured him. "Now about that game . . ."

"Do you play chess?" he asked hopefully.

"I have," she said. To be sure, it had been twenty-four years ago in the third grade, and her enthusiasm hadn't lasted the school year.

"Great! I'll get the pieces." Paul hurried to the sideboard and, opening the bottom drawer, took out a well-polished, mahogany box.

Pleased to have given his thoughts a new direction, Marcy kicked off her shoes and tucked her feet beneath her on the sofa.

Paul cleared the coffee table simply by shoving what appeared to be four antique Meissen shepherdesses to one end.

Marcy gently repositioned the porcelain, then picked up one of the chess pieces he was unpacking. "I want the green ones." She studied the jade queen she was holding with delight.

"Sure, I'll take the ivory." He began to set out his pieces on the board.

Using his placement as a guide, Marcy followed suit, pausing to study the intricate carving on the rook and the tiny rubies that had been used for the bishops' eyes.

"Here, let me help you." Paul finished the job for her. "How good a player are you?"

"Fair, but I should warn you that I haven't played in a while."

"Hmm. Maybe I should give you a piece advantage?"

"How good are *you?*" she countered suspiciously.

"I'm champion of the chess club I belong to," he said.

"Champion?" she repeated weakly. Her idea had been to fill up the half hour until Stephanie came home. At this rate, the game might be over in ten minutes, even if he gave her half a dozen pieces. Unless . . . She felt a smile curve her lips as another idea occurred to her.

"I don't think I'm on your level," she said slowly.

"Very few amateurs are."

"Modest little thing, aren't we?" she said.

"False modesty is not a virtue. Besides, the minute we start to play, you're going to realize how good I am," he added.

And how bad I am, Marcy thought ruefully. "You wouldn't like to play something like Parcheesi, would you?"

"No, I loathe games where so much of the outcome depends on luck, don't you?"

"That depends on whether I have any skill or not," she said dryly. "I'll play chess with you, but I want four of your pieces."

"Four! Why don't I just concede the game?"

"Would you?" she asked curiously.

"I never concede. Anything."

"Inflexibility is a curse," Marcy said primly.

"But persistence is a virtue," he countered.

"In that case I demand four pieces."

Paul studied her for a long moment, then gave her a wicked smile that immediately put her on guard. Finally he said, "All right, but I get to choose the pieces."

"Ha! How dumb do I look? No, don't answer that. I'll compromise. You pick two and I'll pick two."

"Okay," he agreed. "I'll give you two pawns." He picked up two of his pawns and put them back into the box.

Marcy studied the board, trying to recall which pieces did what. All she could remember precisely was that the queen was very important. "For my choices . . .

I'll take your queen and a player to be named later," she said at last.

He frowned at her. "What do you mean—a player to be named later?"

Marcy gave him an innocent look. "Which of those words don't you understand?"

"What I don't understand is your thought process. Exactly how long has it been since you played chess?"

"A little less than a quarter century."

"A quarter—! Do you even remember the moves?"

She raised her eyebrows. "I have an excellent memory. Especially for insults. Do we have a deal?"

"I suppose," he grumbled. "I'll go first."

"Guests are supposed to get to go first," Marcy objected.

"If you'll search that excellent memory of yours, you'll find that white always goes first.'

"You don't have white. You have ivory."

Paul briefly closed his eyes, opened them again and said, "All right, to hell with centuries of tradition. I concede."

"The game?"

"No! The opening move."

"Really." Marcy sniffed. "If you're this touchy, it's a wonder anyone will play with you."

"Just move."

Pleased to have given him something else to think about, Marcy settled down to prolong the game until Stephanie arrived home.

Twenty minutes and one move on her part later, Paul suddenly got to his feet.

Marcy looked up from her study of the board. "Where are you going?"

"To get something to preserve my sanity." He rummaged around in the bottom drawer of the sideboard and pulled out a four-inch-square box.

"What's that?" Marcy asked.

"A timer." He took what looked like a modified clock out of the box, set it on the table beside the chess board and pushed down the brass knob on top. "You have three minutes to make your move. If you don't, you lose your turn."

"Of all the arbitrary...!" she sputtered. "If I rush, I might make a mistake."

"Then you'll learn from your mistakes."

"You mean I'll lose from my mistakes," she grumbled, finally moving a rook.

"You'll lose, anyway," he said simply. Six plays later, it was obvious, even to Marcy's inexperienced eye, that he was right. The outcome was a foregone conclusion. There was no way she could win. Not only was Paul a superb player, he was absolutely ruthless.

Marcy, hoping to postpone the inevitable, moved one of her bishops forward one square, then glanced at Paul to see what he thought of her strategy. He was studying her remaining pieces with a narrow-eyed intensity that she found strangely endearing. As she watched, he reached out, moved his knight and captured her queen.

He gave her a smug smile, pushed in the timer button and said, "Time to make your move."

It certainly was, Marcy thought wryly. She plucked his king from the board, returned his smug smile with interest and announced, "I win."

"You win?" he repeated, incredulous. "You cheated! Put my king back!"

"I did not cheat. Our agreement was that I got a piece to be named later. This is later, and this is the piece." She waved his king at him.

"But you can't take my king. The game is over without the king."

"Very good," Marcy said in a tone of approval. "You know the rules."

"I also know when I've been had. Put my king back."

She laughed. "Are you trying to welsh on our deal? I categorically refuse to allow you to break your word."

Paul eyed her for a long moment, and Marcy felt a quick surge of excitement as the gleam in his eyes deepened.

"Remember what you said about how I should be spontaneous?" he inquired slowly.

"Vaguely," she replied, suddenly cautious.

"Well, I've decided to take a leaf out of my old Boy Scout manual."

"Obviously not the one that deals with clarity. I don't know what you're talking about."

"I have decided that instead of doing one good deed a day, I'll perform one spontaneous act a day."

"Really?"

"Really." He nodded decisively, then, totally without warning, grabbed his king. Marcy instinctively jerked backward in a move than unbalanced both of them. She fell onto the couch with Paul on top of her.

Marcy took a deep breath to steady herself, but it proved a mistake. The feel of his hard body pressing against her was bad enough, but coupled with the tangy scent of his cologne, it was quickly becoming incredibly distracting.

"It's a strange thing about spontaneity," Paul mused, sounding for all the world as if he were giving a lecture in front of one of her classes instead of lying on top of her.

"How so?" Marcy strove for an equally casual tone, hoping to disguise just how *uncasual* she felt inside. She wriggled slightly to try to put a little distance between them, but it didn't work. Her action only seemed to fit them more closely together, and it wasn't long before his legs slipped between hers.

"There are such unexpected consequences. In this case, such very pleasant ones." His voice deepened perceptibly. "You are a very appealing woman, Marcy Handley."

"Mmm, thank you," she murmured.

"And I want very much to kiss you," he whispered.

"Then why don't you?" Marcy abandoned thinking in favor of feeling; at that moment, it seemed a much more rewarding idea.

"Because I'm a lot stronger than you are, you're a guest in my house, and I don't want to take advantage of you."

"You couldn't. I know judo."

His chuckle reverberated through her. "Like you know chess?"

Marcy freed her arms and, reaching up, cupped his face in her hands. "Do you remember what it says in Ecclesiastes about how there's a time for everything?"

He nodded.

"Well, the time for talking is past."

"I see. In that case..." He pushed his fingers through her thick hair, holding her loosely.

Marcy stared into his eyes. They shone softly with the strength of his emotions.

She ran her tongue slowly over her lower lip. As if drawn by the slight movement, his thumb followed its path, rubbing lightly over her mouth.

She inhaled sharply as a sudden shiver chased down her spine. The heat and scent of his body seemed to be overwhelming her, making it difficult for her to think. His thumb moved again, this time probing between her lips and exploring the uneven line of her lower teeth. Her feeling of disorientation grew more intense.

The salty taste of his thumb made her hungry for more. Her eyelids felt heavy; indeed, she was having trouble keeping them open. She wanted to shut out reality so that she could revel in this sensual world, a world where what she felt was the only reality.

You're a sophisticated woman of the world, she tried to tell herself. *You shouldn't be reacting this violently to a simple kiss.* But the message seemed to be coming from far away, from another lifetime. At that moment, nothing about his kiss seemed simple, and she didn't feel sophisticated. She felt vulnerable, extremely vulnerable to this man. What was even more unsettling was that she didn't know why.

"Ah, Marcy..." His husky voice scattered her disquieting thoughts in all directions. "You feel so fantastic."

One hand slipped down to cup her chin, and she watched in breathless anticipation as his lips came closer and closer until they hovered a hairbreadth from her mouth. Finally they brushed her lips. The contact was whisper soft, bringing with it a faint taste of coffee—and total frustration. She felt as if she were attending a banquet and all she'd been offered to eat was a leaf of lettuce drizzled with lemon juice. She wanted to sample the riches around her, wanted to sate herself on them, not be teased by just knowing about them.

Impatient now, Marcy clasped her arms around his neck and tugged him closer, until his mouth met hers again. She relaxed for an infinitesimal second beneath the firm pressure, then tensed as the pressure increased, bringing with it a raging hunger. She felt empty, achingly so.

His tongue touched her lower lip and Marcy shuddered. It was as if she'd jumped off a building and was free-falling to earth.

She tightened her grip and opened her mouth. His seeking tongue found hers and Marcy trembled, feeling goose bumps pop out on her arms.

She twisted slightly, fitting herself still more closely against his hardening body. His reaction was undeniable, but to her intense disappointment, Paul, instead of intensifying their kiss, raised his head and stared at her enigmatically for a long moment.

Marcy reached up and traced the slight frown line between his eyebrows with her finger. What was he thinking? What was he feeling? Did it even begin to approach what she had felt during that brief kiss?

"What's the matter?" she asked softly.

"Nothing." He buried his face in her hair. "You smell so fantastic. Like a whole flower garden. I don't even mind that you cheated."

"I did not cheat." Marcy was determined to follow his lead. "I outwitted you fair and square."

"Ha!" He rolled off her and stood up. "You took advantage of my trusting nature."

"Trusting nature!" Marcy hooted. "Next you'll be telling me that you believe in the tooth fairy."

"Of course I don't." The dimple in his left cheek deepened enticingly. "But I warn you right now I won't hear a word against the Easter Bunny. He's—" The moment of teasing was over. The grandfather clock in the front hall began to chime the hour. Paul counted, frowned, then checked his wristwatch.

"It's twelve o'clock," he said ominously.

"It must be off." It was Marcy's turn to peer at the clock. To her dismay both hands were pointing straight up. Where was Stephanie?

"The only thing off was my judgment, when I agreed to let her go in the first place," Paul declared. All signs of the indulgent lover had disappeared in favor of what Marcy hoped was concern for Stephanie, but feared might just be anger.

"Don't do anything rash," she urged. "Think."

"If I'd been thinking in the first place . . ."

"This is not the time for recriminations. Try calling the school."

"Stephanie said they lock up at ten forty-five, so I doubt that's going to do much good," he objected, but picked up the phone. He punched in the number, listened for what seemed like an interminable time, then hung up.

"It's an answering machine. They suggest calling after seven-thirty tomorrow to talk to a human being. Hell!" He dragged his fingers through his hair. "Seven-thirty may be too late."

"Maybe . . . maybe their car broke down and they're waiting for a tow truck," Marcy suggested.

"That's a possibility." Paul looked hopeful. "I'll go and look—" He broke off at the sound of a key in the front door.

"Car trouble be damned!" He stalked out of the living room with Marcy on his heels. A sweaty, bedraggled-looking Stephanie was in the process of relocking the door.

"Hi," she said tentatively.

"Hi, hell!" Paul roared. "I told you to be home by eleven at the latest and it's midnight."

"I know that!" Stephanie snapped back. "I learned to tell time in kindergarten."

"It's too bad they didn't teach you responsibility at the same time!"

"You're the most hateful—"

"Stop it, both of you!" Marcy yelled.

Stephanie and Paul swung around and stared at her in surprise. If she'd been in the mood to be amused, their expressions would have done the trick. As it was, she was far too annoyed by the way they'd instinctively slipped back into their old, totally unproductive behavior toward each other.

"I'm beginning to wonder if the two of you have listened to a single thing I've said since I got here," she declared, making no attempt to hide her irritation. "Now then," she added when they simply went on staring at her, "if you will both come into the living room, we will discuss this like rational human beings." She turned and marched out of the hallway, hoping they'd follow. To her relief, they did.

Marcy sat down on one of the wing chairs beside the fireplace and waited until Stephanie had flopped onto the sofa and Paul had leaned against the mantel.

"To get back to basics—again—you will each state your position. Paul, you start. Tell Stephanie exactly why you are upset."

"Why I'm upset!" he repeated incredulously.

"*He's* upset?" Stephanie protested.

"Without any editorial comment from either side," Marcy added.

"Very well," he said. "I am upset because Stephanie promised to be home by eleven o'clock and she wasn't."

"Fine. Stephanie, if you would respond to exactly what he said."

Stephanie glared at Paul, gulped and then blurted out, "I couldn't get home by eleven because I promised Mom."

"Promised Hillary what?" Paul demanded.

"That I'd never get into a car with someone who'd been drinking." Stephanie took a deep breath. "You see, Jessie felt kinda sick and so she went home early. Cheryl, one of the seniors who was helping, said that her boyfriend was going to pick her up at ten forty-five and they'd be glad to drop me off because they went right past my house. But when he came to get us, he smelled like the recycling center when they've been processing beer cans." Her nose wrinkled in disgust.

"I told them to go on, that I didn't need a ride, after all, but since everyone else had already left, there wasn't anyone to ride with and the school was already locked and I didn't have any change to use a pay phone. So I had to walk home and it took forever and my feet hurt and you yelled at me!" Her litany of woe ended on a wail.

"Stephanie," Marcy said, "you don't need money to use a pay phone in an emergency. Just push O for the operator and she'll help you."

Paul stared at his niece's flushed face as if he'd never seen her before. A whole range of emotions seethed inside him. Relief that she had had enough common sense not to risk driving with someone who'd been drinking, pride that she had opted for the long walk instead of breaking her word to Hillary, and an overriding urge to throttle Cheryl's boyfriend. But most of all for the first time he felt aware of Stephanie as a person in her own right, not just as an extension of his beloved sister.

"I'm sorry I yelled instead of listening," he said simply. "It's just that I was worried that something had happened to you. That..." He almost choked, remembering the horror of the phone call informing him of his sister's accident.

"I know, Uncle Paul," Stephanie muttered. "I worry, too, when people are late, but I honestly didn't know what else to do."

"You did exactly the right thing in not getting into that car," he said emphatically.

"Thank you," she said, giving Marcy an uncertain glance.

"Your uncle is right," Marcy added. "You handled the situation with a great deal of maturity. Your mother would have been proud of you."

"Thank you," Stephanie whispered. "I guess I'd better get to bed, then." She scooted up the stairs.

Paul sighed as she disappeared from view. "I blew that one."

"No, you didn't." Marcy wanted to wipe away his bleak expression. He looked so alone. She wanted to put her arms around him and tell him that everything would be all right. Even though she wasn't sure it was true.

"But I yelled when I should have listened to her," he berated himself.

"Yes, and hopefully next time you'll remember and listen first, yell second."

He grimaced. "I'm beginning to wonder if I have what it takes to be a parent."

"Of course you do. Just remember that most people get to learn parenting with a baby. And the great thing about babies is that it's years before they can talk."

A rueful smile lifted Paul's lips. "Thanks. I'll try to keep that in mind."

"I don't know about you, but all this on top of the chess game has tired me out. I'm going up to bed."

"I don't know how you can sleep with a guilty conscience."

"Nobody likes a sore loser." Marcy threw the words over her shoulder as she sprinted up the stairs. When she reached the top, she looked back. Paul was still standing there, watching her. Her eyes met his, and she felt a curious sensation, as if she were being pulled back down the stairs toward him. She blinked to break the spell, but had to force her feet to move away.

She paused outside Stephanie's door, but all was quiet, so she continued to her own room, pleased with her evening. Not only had she gotten a fair amount of work done on her book, but she had had a pleasant time playing chess with Paul. And a mind-blowing kiss. And to cap it all, Paul had learned a valuable lesson about dealing with his niece, one she rather suspected he wouldn't forget. He was a very astute man. Usually. She giggled, remembering the expression on his face when she'd confiscated his king.

There was no doubt about it. Paul Wycoff was an incredibly appealing man. She sank onto her bed, in the mood for dreams. In fact, he was one of the most appealing men she'd ever met, and she was looking forward to getting to know him better. A whole lot better. She shivered in anticipation.

THAT DELICIOUS FEELING that something wonderful was about to happen was still there when Marcy woke up the next morning, rather like the feeling she'd had as a child when Christmas was approaching. She rushed through her dressing, eager to get downstairs and spend a few minutes with Paul before he left for the office. And tomorrow was Saturday, which meant a whole weekend free, she thought eagerly.

Marcy paused in the doorway of the oversize kitchen, her eyes homing in on Paul. He was seated alone at the breakfast table, reading the morning paper.

Marcy studied him. What was it exactly about him that affected her so strongly? He was handsome, but nowhere near as handsome as the history professor she'd dated last year. He was in good physical shape, but didn't begin to compare with the assistant football coach she'd dated over the summer. He was certainly intelligent, but then, so were the vast majority of men she met at the university. So why was Paul different? No answer immediately leaped to mind.

Paul felt a shimmer of some indefinable emotion and, frowning at the unexpected sensation, turned around. He found himself smiling when he saw Marcy. He should have known, he thought ruefully. She'd been disturbing his sense of peace ever since he'd met her.

He watched her cross the kitchen toward him. The bright morning sunlight pouring from the skylights added a reddish haze to her hair and a golden sheen to her smooth skin, giving her the air of a beam of sunlight that had somehow been imbued with human life.

Marcy slipped into the chair across from him and gave him a cheerful smile. She poured herself a cup of coffee from the pot on the table and took a sip.

"Have you—?" She paused. A sudden clatter of footsteps on the back stairs heralded Stephanie's arrival.

"Good morning!" Stephanie hurriedly poured herself a glass of orange juice and in between gulps began to stuff fruit into the knapsack she was carrying.

"Sit down and eat a proper breakfast," Paul said. "It won't matter if you're late, for once."

"You have obviously not met our dean of students, or you'd never say that," Stephanie said. "Everything matters to her. Besides, when you go into the room late, everyone turns and stares at you."

"Oh, I see," Paul said, not seeing at all. "But before you cut out of here, tell me what we should do for a present for Aunt Clementia's birthday."

Stephanie grimaced. "Your guess is as good as mine. I asked her what she wanted last week, and she said just my best wishes, which was totally useless. I want to get her something really special."

"The question is, what?" Paul repeated. "It gets harder every year. She already has everything she wants. Or needs, for that matter."

Marcy looked thoughtful. "You know, I think the problem is that you two are thinking in terms of material gifts."

"Mom used to give Dad a coupon book for his birthday, good for things like hugs and free Saturdays and . . ." Stephanie's voice trailed away into silence.

Paul, remembering that Marcy had said not talking about his sister was depriving Stephanie of her memories, dredged up a few memories of his own. "Your mother started doing that after she read an article in a magazine when she was in college. I must have been about six at the time. That Christmas she gave me ten coupons and said I could give her one anytime she was yelling at me and she'd instantly shut up. She honored them, too. And after I'd used them all up, I snuck into her room while she was out one night, stole them out of her desk and reused them. And she never let on that she knew what I'd done."

"She sounds like quite a woman." Marcy gave him a warm, encouraging smile.

"Yes, she was," Stephanie whispered and made a production out of drinking her juice.

"What you two ought to do is apply Hillary's idea to your aunt's present," Marcy suggested.

"You mean like doing something for Aunt Clementia?" Stephanie asked uncertainly.

"Or maybe by getting her something personal that she'd really like," Paul said slowly. "Something like…a séance?"

"What a wonderful idea!" Stephanie stared at him with open approval. "She'll love it, especially if you can manage to produce a spirit or two."

"Spirits are where I draw the line," Paul said.

"But Uncle Paul, what's a ghost or two if you're already doing the séance?" Stephanie was clearly taken by the idea. "Aunt Clementia will love a ghost. Just think."

"I am," he said dryly. "And I refuse to insult her intelligence by producing a fraud. I know that sounds like I'm splitting hairs, considering the fact that I don't believe that séances are anything but frauds, but there's a difference."

A car horn sounded. "Uh-oh. That'll be Jessie's mom," Stephanie said. She grabbed her knapsack and sprinted for the kitchen door. "See you tonight. I think we ought to go for the séance, Uncle Paul."

Paul turned to Marcy as the door slammed shut behind her. "Tell me. How does one go about setting up a séance?"

"By calling in an expert, of course." Marcy reached for the newspaper and turned to the want ads. She quickly found the Personals column and ran her finger down the page.

She paused halfway down. "Aha! Pay dirt. Here we are. Madame Zola. Palms read. Futures disclosed. Call 555-2167 for an appointment."

Paul stared into her sparkling eyes for a moment, then said, "It's morning."

"Yes?" Marcy gave him a puzzled look.

"And I haven't used up my impulsive gesture for the day."

"Oh?" Marcy eyed him with sudden interest.

"I could spend it checking out this Madame Zola with you," he suggested tentatively. "There's nothing going on at work that won't wait."

"You're on." Marcy beamed at him. She took the paper and walked to the phone.

"What are you doing?" Paul asked as she began to punch in a number.

"Setting up an appointment to get your palm read."

"*My* palm! What's wrong with your palm?"

"I can't do everything myself. Besides, you're an obvious skeptic. I want to see how this Madame Zola handles you."

Paul watched Marcy's animated expression as she began to talk to whoever had answered the phone. If it ever got out that he'd gone to get his palm read, his friends would probably still be ribbing him about it at his retirement party.

"Well," he asked the minute she hung up, "what'd she say?"

"We have an appointment for a reading in exactly—" she checked her watch "—thirty-five minutes. How long will it take us to get there?"

"That rather depends on where we're going."

Marcy told him and he tried to place the location. "That's across town. Even on the expressway it'll take a good half hour at this time of day. We'll need to leave immediately."

"No problem. I'm almost finished with my morning dose of caffeine." She gulped down the rest of her coffee, then poured a fresh cupful to drink on the way.

As PAUL HAD PREDICTED, it took them all of thirty-five minutes to reach the address Madam Zola had given them. Marcy studied the small, shabby frame house with a critical eye. The dingy white paint was peeling from the weathered boards, and the porch that ran the length of the front was listing at one end. One of the panes of glass in the window to the right of the battered door had been broken, and a faded red rag had been stuffed into the hole. Litter was scattered around the small, dirt-packed yard as if it had rained trash sometime in the past and no one had bothered to pick it up.

"You'd think a person who professes to read the future could pick herself a few winners at the track and move to a more confidence-inspiring location," Paul said.

"It's probably rented," Marcy decided. "Come on. Let's go see."

The door swung open as they approached, to reveal a thin woman of indeterminate age, who stood at least six-three. Marcy blinked. Bright sunlight glittered off a profusion of gold chains the woman was wearing around her neck. A spotless yellow silk blouse covered her flat chest, and a brilliant magenta cotton skirt almost reached her bare feet.

"Madame Zola?" Marcy asked when Paul remained silent.

"Yes. And you are the one who called earlier. I recognize your vibrations."

"And her voice," Paul said dryly.

"Ah, do I detect an unbeliever?" Madame Zola eyed him dispassionately.

"Let's just say I have reservations," Paul told her.

"No matter." Madame Zola waved them inside in a regal manner totally at variance with her shabby surroundings. Paul sneezed as he breathed in the overpowering scent of incense, which hung in the air like a cloud.

"Sit," Madame Zola commanded, and Marcy obediently sank onto the faded crimson sofa. Paul sat down a little more gingerly. The final, farcical touch would be for the sofa to collapse beneath them. To his relief, it held firm.

"Now, then. How may I use my talents on your behalf?" Madame Zola asked.

"I want you to read his palm." Marcy nodded to Paul. "I should warn you that he's a skeptic."

"Unnecessary," Madame Zola said. "Fortunately, my talents do not depend on his belief. Your hand, my good man." She gestured imperiously.

Paul obeyed, and Madame Zola stared at his palm for a long moment. Finally she spoke. "You have a very long lifeline. Very strong." She glanced at Marcy. "You were, perhaps, wondering what kind of lover he'd be?"

"No," Marcy replied. But an image of Paul without the civilizing effect of clothes fluttered through her mind.

"Ah!" Madame Zola nodded sagely. "It is more than just sex, then. It is a husband you are thinking of. You are wise to seek my advice."

Marcy opened her mouth to deny the suggestion, then her curiosity got the better of her. Though Paul looked simply incredulous, she asked, "What's your advice?"

"Proceed with extreme caution. He is very different from you."

"It doesn't get any more different than a man and a woman," Paul said, beginning to enjoy himself.

"Ah, but what man for what woman?" Madame Zola countered. She turned to Marcy. "This man would make an excellent provider. Never would you know want, which is not a factor to be lightly dismissed. His standing in the community is assured, and he will never do anything to jeopardize it. Also—"

"There's one other thing." Marcy cut her off, afraid things might get too personal. Paul was being a good sport about all this, but there had to be a limit to his tolerance, and she didn't want to reach it before they had everything arranged. "Do you do private parties?"

Madame Zola's eyes narrowed speculatively. "That depends," she said finally.

"On what?" Paul asked.

"On the aura," Madame Zola intoned. "The spirits must be in accord."

"I sure hope they are," Marcy said. "You see, this coming Thursday is his aunt's eightieth birthday, and she is very interested in the supernatural. Not so much palm reading as crystal ball reading."

"Ah, a soul mate." Madame Zola beamed.

"What we want you to do, Madame Zola, is to hold a séance," Marcy told her.

"You do realize, do you not, that it takes great talent as well as tremendous effort to reach the spirit world. I would be exhausted afterward for days, perhaps even weeks."

"It isn't all that long a trip," Paul countered, recognizing her words as the opening gambit in a business deal.

He saw Marcy frown at him. "Naturally we would expect to compensate you accordingly," he added hastily.

"Is there any particular spirit you wish me to contact?" Madame Zola asked.

"Yes, Caleb Wycoff," Paul told her. "Aunt Clementia adores the old reprobate."

"An ancestor of yours?" Madame Zola eyed him attentively, and Paul swallowed a sigh; his impulsive words had undoubtedly given his identity away. The fee had probably just doubled.

"Yes," he answered. "Caleb is Aunt Clementia's favorite, which has to be the classic example of opposites attracting."

"Why?" Marcy wanted to know.

"Because Caleb Wycoff was a self-serving, immoral, unprincipled bastard, and that was on his good days, of which, from all accounts, he had few," Paul told her.

"I doubt that many great fortunes were amassed by considerate men playing by the rules," Marcy said mildly.

"They still aren't!" Madame Zola's accent slipped for a second and she sounded pure south Boston. "Now, then," she went on in the tone she had used before, "as to this séance of yours, I cannot possibly do it for less than five hundred dollars."

"Five hundred dollars!" Paul repeated.

"And cab fare," Madame Zola added prosaically. "Talent like mine doesn't come cheap.'

"At that price it isn't likely to come at all!" Paul warned.

"If you want a bargain, go to a discount store," Madame Zola said. "I am an artiste."

Paul looked at Marcy, letting his eyes linger on the line of her soft lips before moving his gaze to her laughing eyes. Despite his instinctive dislike of being ripped off, he knew he was going to agree. It was worth the five hundred dollars just to keep the laughter in Marcy's eyes.

"All right," he said. "Five hundred and cab fare. But I'll pay you after the séance."

"That is acceptable." Madame Zola nodded majestically. "And since you pay as you go, I assume you wish to pay today's fee now?"

"How much?" Paul asked.

"Twenty dollars. Leave it in the crystal bowl beside the door as you leave." She sank onto the decrepit chair across from them and wearily closed her eyes. "My efforts on your behalf have exhausted me. I must rest and recoup my energies for Thursday."

"Of course, Madame Zola." Marcy got to her feet and the two of them left.

Once he'd pulled onto the expressway, he said, "That woman is a con artist."

"Only in the sense that all actresses are. You pay them to create a fantasy world that you can share for a brief span of time. And Madame Zola appears to be a very astute judge of human nature. From the looks of her act this morning, I think she'll give Clementia a memorable performance. I'll also lay you odds that by Thursday she'll know more about Caleb Wycoff than you do."

"And none of it'll be good." He lapsed into silence, concentrating on navigating them safely through the bumper-to-bumper traffic that clogged the highway.

"Do you suppose Madame Zola will want her money in plain, unmarked bills?" he asked Marcy when they reached home.

Marcy chuckled. "In cash, at least."

"What do you have planned for the rest of the day? Not another meal?" he inquired, suddenly remembering that Mrs. Bailey was still sick.

Marcy chuckled again, this time at his apprehensive expression. "Where's your spirit of culinary adventure?"

"Dead," he said succinctly. "The sight of that stuff you called tofu killed it."

"You didn't even try it, and you should have. It's not half bad."

"It's probably all bad," he muttered.

"Well, set your mind at rest. If Mrs. Bailey isn't back today, I'll throw her roast in the oven because I don't have time to be creative. I'm planning on working on my book." *And making a few phone calls to various colleagues*, she added for her own benefit.

"What kind of book are you writing?" he asked, remembering that he wasn't supposed to know anything about it. That bit of information had come from the detective agency.

"Nonfiction, about what a woman should wear to project the kind of image she wants. It's based on some research I did last year."

"I hired a consulting firm to come in and give a workshop for my staff on that subject last winter."

"Was the firm located here in Boston?"

"No, I couldn't find anyone in the area who did that kind of work. They were from New York City."

"How did it go?" she asked curiously.

"The men felt it was really helpful, but the reaction of the women was much more mixed. Most of them said his information was heavily slanted toward the man in the gray flannel suit."

"They could well be right. Women have traditionally been second-class citizens in the workplace."

"Not in mine," Paul objected. "The base salary at my firm is the same for everyone, and bonuses are standard."

"I didn't mean that personally," Marcy explained. "I was simply stating a general fact."

"Would you consider giving a workshop for the women on my staff?"

"I'd like to do that," she said slowly. What a terrific chance to add to her material!

6

"I'M HOME. Anybody here?" Paul called from the front door. His excitement was growing. He wanted to see Marcy and tell her how enthusiastic the women on his staff were about the workshop idea.

Seeing the living room was empty, he checked the study. Other than a pile of Marcy's scribbled notes on the desk, there was no sign of her.

Disappointment nibbled at his sense of anticipation. Where could she be at five o'clock? Frowning, he headed for the kitchen, hoping she'd be there.

She was. And so was Stephanie.

"Oh, Uncle Paul!" she wailed.

"What's the matter?" Paul felt a quick clutch of fear at Stephanie's woebegone expression. "Aunt Clementia?" He took a step toward the back door.

"Is fine," Marcy said firmly. "I had tea with her not two hours ago. She's trying to teach me to read the leaves. There's a whole lot more to it than you might think."

"How can you talk about tea leaves at a time like this?" Stephanie demanded.

"A time like what?" Paul asked, feeling calmer now that he knew everyone was safe.

"Vanessa Hargrave brought to school a picture of the dress she's going to wear to the dance tomorrow night, and it's the same as mine," Stephanie moaned. "Exactly."

"Well, there'll be a couple of hundred people there," Paul pointed out. "No one will notice."

"Of course they will. And not only that, but Vanessa Hargrave is gorgeous, absolutely gorgeous," she lamented.

"So are you," Paul said sincerely. "You have a beautiful smile and—"

"*Smile!*" Stephanie stared at him as if he had lost his mind. "Vanessa Hargrave has ash blond hair, a perfect complexion, green eyes, a great figure, and what's even worse, she's nice."

Paul stared back at her, but when she didn't add anything more, he looked questioningly at Marcy.

"You can't dislike someone who's nice," Marcy explained. "If you do, you feel guilty."

"That I understand," Paul said. "The rest escapes me."

"I just told you!" Stephanie exclaimed. "If you'd been listening—"

"I think we ought to work on solutions," Marcy broke in. "Not in trying to apportion blame."

"I take it my idea of pretending not to notice isn't going to fly?" Paul asked.

Marcy gave him a pitying look. "It isn't even going to make it off the ground."

"Jessie said she'd loan me her dress from last winter's Valentine's Day Dance, but it's purple. Dark purple."

"Not your color," Marcy agreed.

"Is there any reason why we can't just buy a new dress?" Paul asked in confusion.

"The dance is tomorrow. Everything will be picked over," Stephanie said gloomily.

Marcy seconded Paul's suggestion. "Boston's a big place."

"But—"

"You could be right that you won't find anything," Marcy said quickly, "but you could also be wrong. Why don't we go see?"

"Well . . ." It was Stephanie's turn to frown. "I don't have to be at the football game tonight until eight."

"That's over three hours away," Paul said. "You two ought to be able to cover the mall by then."

"We *two*?" Marcy eyed him narrowly. "Since when did you opt out?"

"Me?" Paul blinked. "I'm a man."

"Very good." Marcy nodded approvingly while Stephanie giggled. "Now what does that have to do with it? You aren't going to try on some stereotypical sex roles, are you?"

Paul grinned. "The thought had crossed my mind. I don't know anything about shopping."

"So learn." Marcy was clearly unsympathetic. "Besides, you can drive. The traffic's horrendous."

"You could learn," he said slyly.

"Ah, but I'd have to learn to use a stick shift in your car. Your dent-free, S-class Mercedes-Benz."

Paul shuddered. "Never mind, I surrender. I'll go and I'll drive."

"You mean it, Uncle Paul?"

"Sure, we'll find you the most gorgeous dress left in Boston."

"Thank you!" Stephanie threw her arms around him and gave him a quick hug. "I'll get my purse and be right back." She skipped out of the room.

Paul gave Marcy a rueful glance. "I think this comes under the heading of, 'If it weren't for the honor, I'd just as soon pass.'"

Marcy chuckled. "Nonsense, you'll love it."

HER PROPHECY FELL WIDE of the mark. Paul did not enjoy it. Not the mindless idiots trying to sideswipe him in the parking lot, nor the hordes of shoppers who surged around him as they entered the mall, and he most emphatically didn't enjoy the sight of his niece gazing covetously at a black silk slither of a dress that left very little to the imagination.

He glanced at Marcy, who was listening to Stephanie's rhapsodizing. Surely she didn't approve of that provocative thing? He couldn't tell by her expression. She might simply be letting Stephanie talk herself out, or planning to let the girl make her own mistakes. He decided to take no risks.

Picking out a delightful confection in soft pink, he offered it to Stephanie. "This is pretty," he suggested.

"Oh, Uncle Paul, it has ruffles," Stephanie said disparagingly.

Uncertain as to what her comment implied, he decided not to push the issue. There were, after all, plenty of dresses to choose from. He reached for another that looked fine to him. "How about this one?"

"It's still pink." This time Stephanie wrinkled her nose in disgust.

"Okay." He took a deep breath. "No pink and no ruffles. How about this one?" He pulled out a yellow taffeta with a gauze overskirt.

"Too juvenile," she pronounced.

"But, Stephanie, you *are* a juvenile," he pointed out, then wished he hadn't when he saw Marcy wince.

"Though you're very mature for your age," he added, trying to make amends.

"I am *not* juvenile!" Now Stephanie was glaring at him again.

"I think you'd better quit while you're not too far behind," Marcy told him, her eyes brimming with suppressed laughter.

"I want that black dress." Stephanie pointed to the one that horrified Paul. "It's my dance and my choice."

"You forget that it's my money," he retorted.

"You would be so despicable as to use money to force your . . . your disgustingly infantile taste on me!" She gestured toward the maligned yellow dress.

"The thought had occurred to me," Paul said. "Sooner or later everyone has to learn that he who pays the piper calls the tune."

"I'd rather go as a second-class clone of Vanessa than succumb to blackmail!" Stephanie said melodramatically.

"Does Madame require any help?" A salesclerk materialized from behind a rack of evening blouses, addressing her question to Marcy.

"Not at the moment, thank you. We're going to get a cup of coffee, and then we'll decide which ones we want to try on."

"I've already decided," Stephanie grumbled.

"You might try the coffee shop in the basement," the clerk suggested.

"Thank you." Marcy smiled at the woman and, taking Paul's arm, started toward the escalators. Behind them he could hear Stephanie muttering to herself.

Stephanie managed to contain herself until they'd been served, then blurted, "I want that dress!"

"No!" Paul shot back.

"I wish the pair of you would remember the drill for handling arguments," Marcy said tiredly.

"But—" Stephanie began again.

Marcy gave her a level look, and Stephanie lapsed into a sulky silence. Turning to him, Marcy said, "Tell Stephanie why you are opposed to that dress."

"Because it looks like something I'd expect to find a high-priced hooker wearing, not my fifteen-year-old niece."

"You have a dirty mind!" Stephanie snapped.

"No personal comments," Marcy said. "Stick to the facts."

"The fact is he has—"

"Stephanie," Marcy warned.

"But he really can't expect me to wear one of those things he picked out. They're so . . ." She grimaced.

"So what?" Marcy persisted. "If you want him to understand your point of view, you have to put what you think into words. Your uncle's not a mind reader."

Stephanie giggled unexpectedly. "No, that's Aunt Clementia, isn't it? Uncle Paul, there's nothing wrong with those dresses, but they look like something a kid in junior high would wear. Too sweet for words. Don't you see?"

"No," Paul said honestly, "but I'll take your word for it. Is it the color of the dresses you object to or the style?" He felt a glow of satisfaction as Marcy gave him an approving nod. It was strange; when she'd first arrived, he'd thought she would be an obstacle in the way of making friends with Stephanie. But it was turning out to be just the opposite. Marcy was showing him both what he'd been doing wrong, and how to fix it.

Stephanie pursed her lips, thought a moment and finally said, "I hate ruffles and pastels. The rest is okay."

"What color do you like?" Paul asked.

"Black. I love black," she said enthusiastically. "It's so sophisticated."

He had to struggle to keep back his retort.

"And that black dress . . ." she went on.

"I'll give up on the pink ruffles if you'll give up on that thing," he offered hurriedly.

"Well . . ." Stephanie sighed, then agreed. "All right, but I get black."

"Okay, black it is." Paul was rather surprised to have gained his point without more of a fight. This method of Marcy's wasn't just good, it was fantastic.

"Great! Let's hurry, then! I don't want to be late for the football game. Some of the kids who helped with the decorating asked Jessie and me to sit with them." Stephanie got to her feet and Marcy, taking a last hasty sip of her coffee, followed suit.

"You did well," she whispered to Paul as Stephanie headed up the escalator.

"Thank you," Paul whispered back. "I'm beginning to think parenting is like sailing. You just need to get your sea legs."

Marcy chuckled. "And watch out for squalls that suddenly blow up out of a clear blue sky."

"You should have some kids of your own," Paul said thoughtfully.

"Some?"

"My best friend when I was a kid was the youngest of nine children. I always thought he was the luckiest devil."

"I wonder if his mother thought so," Marcy said dryly.

Paul frowned. "Don't you want more children?"

She forced herself to ignore the "more," and responded to the basic question. "Sure I do. But two would be plenty as far as I'm concerned."

"Two isn't very many."

"Enough is as good as a feast," Marcy said, quoting her grandmother's favorite proverb. She stepped off the escalator and headed toward Stephanie, who was happily rummaging through a rack of black dresses. What would Paul's children be like? she wondered, surreptitiously studying him. He had stopped beside an elaborate, sequined evening gown and was clearly trying to look as if he knew what he was doing.

Would his children have his lean, chiseled features and dark eyes? His tantalizing smile, or that dimple in his left cheek that peeped out when he laughed?

Stephanie interrupted her fanciful musings. "Marcy, what do you think about this one?"

She studied the dress Stephanie was holding up. It had a simply cut, black lace strapless top, attached to a full black taffeta skirt.

"Looks great on the hanger," she said. "Why don't you try it on?"

"Come help?" Stephanie asked.

"Sure. We'll be right back, Paul."

"Take your time," he said, trying not to look as ill at ease as he felt.

Fortunately, the dress proved to be a perfect fit and Stephanie reappeared within minutes to hand it to the hovering salesclerk.

"Does Miss have a matching evening purse?" the clerk asked Stephanie.

"No, the only one I have is green and white," she replied.

"Possibly not the best choice," the clerk said diplomatically. "You might want to try the handbags in our shoe department on your way downstairs."

"Shoes! Marcy, I don't have any shoes that will match, either."

"Easily remedied," Marcy said soothingly. "We'll find something on our way out."

The something Stephanie found had five-inch silver heels. Paul watched her wobble across the carpet and was reminded of the old saying about an accident waiting to happen.

He glanced at Marcy and found her watching him. She nodded ever so slightly. Encouraged, he said, "That silver color is a good choice with the black dress, Stephanie."

"Yes, isn't it?" Stephanie slightly raised one foot to better admire the shoe and almost fell over. "I just need to practice walking in them for a while."

For about four years, Paul thought. How could he persuade her to set her sights lower—about three inches lower? Recalling his own teenage years, he said casually, "Boys must be taller on average than they were when I was your age."

Stephanie looked blank. "Why?"

"If you can wear heels that high and still be shorter than most of the boys in your class . . . I remember how I used to hate having to dance with girls who were taller than me."

Stephanie frowned. "That's silly."

"Sure it is," Paul agreed promptly. "Now I know looks aren't that important. But at sixteen my ego was a very fragile thing, especially where girls were concerned. . . . While you're deciding about your shoes, I'll be across the aisle in leather goods. I need a new briefcase," he added, giving her a chance to change her mind without appearing to yield. If she didn't . . .

He grimaced. There were many worse things that could happen than falling over her feet in those shoes and spraining an ankle, he reminded himself.

But to his relief, when Stephanie and Marcy rejoined him a few minutes later, Stephanie said, "I decided to get lower heels, Uncle Paul. There aren't all that many boys who dance well. I don't want to discourage anyone over anything as silly as who's taller."

"Wise choice," Marcy agreed. "Now that we've taken care of that, I'm starved. Why don't we head for home? There's all that leftover tofu I could heat up for us."

"I wouldn't dream of putting you to the trouble," Paul assured her.

Stephanie hurried to support him. "Let's eat at a restaurant on our way back."

"Excellent idea." Paul ushered them through the main exit. "We can stop off at Ruffles. They do an excellent prime rib."

"Somehow that doesn't surprise me," Marcy said dryly. Honestly, the pair of them were as bad as Pavlov's dogs. All she had to do was mention a healthy meat substitute and they drew together like a wagon train on the prairie, circling to ward off an attack.

Marcy slipped into the front seat of the Mercedes, fastened the seat belt and reviewed their shopping expedition. Paul was making real strides in learning how to set limits for Stephanie. If only she, Marcy, were making equal strides in solving her own problems!

She swallowed a sigh. Despite her phone calls to various members of the department, trying to minimize the damage Bill Sidney's gossip had caused, she could almost feel the support of several key people slipping away. And what was worse, she didn't know how to stop the slide. All she could do right now was wait for Daniel to get back to her with the results of his analysis of those signatures. Once she had the facts, she could respond to Bill Sidney's lies. She just hoped it wouldn't be too late.

In the meantime, she could work on her book, though even that wasn't going according to plan. She stole a quick glance at Paul as he fearlessly aimed the Mercedes at a minuscule opening in the heavy traffic. He was beginning to preoccupy her to an alarming degree. It was the first time a man—any man—had been able to distract her from her work, and it nagged at her because she didn't know why he affected her so strangely. Nor did she know if the feeling was reciprocated. Not that it really mattered. After all, once they found out who the girl's biological mother was, she would leave, and the only times she would see Paul would probably be when he dropped Stephanie off for family gatherings. All she needed to do was figure out a way to banish Paul from her mind when she was working.

SHE WAS DETERMINED to do just that after Stephanie left for the football game that evening. She tried every concentration technique she knew but still couldn't oust him from her thoughts.

Marcy squinted at the row of numbers that marched across the page, trying to bring them into focus. But her eyes weren't really the problem. It was her mind. She simply wasn't all that interested in describing how different age groups of college-educated males had reacted to women wearing red, gray and dark blue wool suits.

She glanced at Paul, who was sitting across from her. He was sifting through an impressive stack of legal-size paper, which he'd spread all over the coffee table. It didn't look any more interesting than her own work.

She shifted in the chair as the clock struck nine-thirty. "How long do football games last?" she asked.

Paul looked up. "You mean high school games?"

"Uh-huh."

"If their team's previous record is any indication, the game, for all practical purposes, will be over in the first five minutes."

"They can't be that bad."

"They're worse," Paul said succinctly. "They lost their first game sixty-nine to nothing and their second eighty to zero. Tonight is their third."

Marcy winced. "The progression of the scores is not encouraging."

"Especially not when you consider that they play ten games," he said wryly. "It's a good thing Stephanie only goes there to be with her friends."

"What's her curfew tonight?"

"Eleven. There's no school tomorrow. Jessie's parents are going, and they offered to drop off Stephanie afterward."

He moved a few more papers from one stack to another, eyed her speculatively for a few seconds, then said, "I haven't used my spontaneous act for the day, and it's getting late."

"Better late than never," Marcy said encouragingly.

"And I was thinking . . ."

"Now that's a promising beginning."

"That we could go for a walk in the rain."

Marcy blinked. "What rain?"

"It's sprinkling outside. Hadn't you noticed?"

No, Marcy thought ruefully. She'd been so busy trying to pretend she wasn't watching Paul that she hadn't noticed what the weather was doing.

"Tell me," she said, "does a walk in the rain constitute a whole spontaneous act or is it part of a sequence?"

Paul rubbed his index finger over his jawline and Marcy shivered, almost feeling the raspy texture of his emerging beard.

"That depends on how things fall out," he said. "It could be part of a sequence."

Marcy's excitement intensified. "You're on. Where are we walking to?"

"Just around the grounds. If Aunt Clementia's lights are on, we can have a cup of tea with her and listen to her patented lecture on how most illnesses are caused by wet feet."

Marcy chuckled. "What if she's already gone to bed?"

He gave her a wicked grin. "I'm adaptable."

He was becoming damn near irresistible, Marcy thought with a faint feeling of unease, which she nonetheless refused to examine. She tossed her papers onto the coffee table; he got to his feet.

"Do we take an umbrella?" she asked.

"Nope. Too much planning ruins spontaneity. We'll tough it out."

She fell happily into step beside him. Suddenly, the world had become a fascinating place, full of all kinds of possibilities.

As they left the sanctuary of the house and stepped into the warm, wet darkness of the night, raindrops pelted Marcy's bare head and dripped down her neck. She squinted up and received a faceful of raindrops for her trouble.

"You know," she mused, "I can't remember the last time I went walking in the rain."

"Me, either." Paul took her hand. "It was probably when I was a kid. But I'm beginning to think I wasted my day's spontaneous gesture. In the movies, it's always romantic." He shook his head, scattering the

clinging droplets that glittered in his hair like dia-
monds.

Marcy peered at him through the darkness, her gaze
lingering on the slick sheen the rain gave to his skin.

"Personally, I'm finding it very wet." She grinned at
him. "But I'm willing to be convinced about the romantic part."

"It's a freeing experience," Paul said.

"Have you been reading psychology books?" Marcy
asked suspiciously, but Paul emphatically denied the
charge.

Stepping into a puddle, he yelped in shock when his
shoes were flooded with muddy water, then he sneezed.

Marcy giggled. "I think the only things being freed
are the germs. Aunt Clementia's lights are out. You
want to go back to the house?"

. He refused to give up so easily. "No." Instead, he
searched his mind for a suitable topic of conversation,
but nothing occurred to him. He couldn't seem to get
beyond the feeling that his wet socks were being eaten
by his shoes.

Marcy stopped abruptly when they reached Clementia's flower moat and sniffed appreciatively. "You
can smell the flowers."

"Smells like damp earth to me. In fact, after all your
talk of the supernatural, it reminds me of crypts and
vampires." His voice deepened. "And wooden stakes.
Or is it silver bullets?"

Marcy shuddered. "Stop that. What's funny in broad
daylight isn't the least bit funny in the dark."

"Or under a full moon," he intoned.

Marcy looked at the sky. "You can't even see the moon."

"But I know it's full." He gave her a wide grin, enjoying himself immensely. "It's in my blood."

"What? Insanity?"

"No, the supernatural." He reached out, intending to kiss her, but his sudden movement must have startled her, because she jerked back. For a fraction of a second she teetered on the edge of the moat, then the wet earth crumbled and she fell backward.

Paul tried to grab her, but all he caught was her blouse. The sound of tearing fabric echoed in the still night air, immediately overlaid by his muffled curse at his own clumsiness.

Marcy landed on her back on a dense carpet of marigolds. As she sank into the soft cushion, the pungent odor of the crushed flowers assailed her nostrils.

More flowers were sacrificed as Paul scrambled into the moat after her. He dropped to his knees beside her.

The glow from the porch light beside Clementia's front door bathed Marcy's face in a pearly radiance, and the bright yellow marigolds behind her head seemed to take on an unearthly air. She looked like a pagan sacrifice.

Marcy reached up and lightly stroked her fingers over his jawline. He held his breath, afraid to move for fear of breaking the spell.

"Paul?" Her whisper seemed to echo in his ears. He stared down. The raindrops made her mouth look soft and wet. As he watched, she ran her tongue over the drops, wiping them away.

He lightly touched his mouth to hers, and the tip of her tongue darted out to explore the fullness of his lower lip. Bathed in a glow of sensation, it felt as if he'd never kissed a woman before. Certainly he'd never kissed one before who'd had this effect on him.

He pressed harder and her lips opened wider. He pushed his tongue into her mouth, grasped the cool softness of her chin in his fingers, then began to cover her face with light kisses. Slowly, meticulously, he kissed every inch of her face. The light floral fragrance she was wearing temporarily replaced the scent of the marigolds.

Next year, Paul thought distractedly, he'd try to convince his aunt to plant some other type of flowers. Ones that didn't give off quite such a strong odor when you rolled around in them.

His lips discovered the vein throbbing in Marcy's right temple. He could actually feel her blood pounding, echoing the fierce rhythm of his own heartbeat. He raised his head slightly to bring her features into focus. Her eyes were closed, her long lashes shadows against her pale skin. Her lips were still parted, and he could hear her drawing breath in labored gulps.

A deep sense of satisfaction filled him at the sight of her intense absorption. He brushed his mouth over her eyelashes, feeling them flutter. His lips continued their odyssey to her mouth, where he nibbled lightly on her lower lip.

He could feel the hunger growing inside, becoming an urgent need to get closer, to submerge himself in her.

His gaze dropped to her smooth, velvety skin, visible between the ripped edges of her blouse. He swallowed hard at the sight of her breasts, barely covered by the flimsy scrap of lace that masqueraded as underwear. Trembling, he reached out and reverently laid a hand over one breast. The heat from her skin warmed his chilled fingers, then he felt her nipple harden into a tight bud of desire that burned against his palm.

He could feel each and every one of his muscles tense in an agony of anticipation and expelled his breath on a long, shaky sigh, trying to control his reactions. He wanted to tell her how beautiful she was. How incredibly sexy. How fantastically alive she made him feel. But he was afraid. The scene had a magical, otherworldly quality that speech would destroy.

Paul lowered his head again and gently began to graze her nipple through the lace with his lips, feeling a surge of power when she jerked violently in response. Lord, but he wanted to make love to her. Not here, though, in the mud and crushed flowers.

"Marcy," he whispered hoarsely, "I want to make love to you. If you want . . ."

"Yes," she murmured. "I do want. Very much."

"Come on, then. Let's go back." Taking her hand, he pulled her to her feet.

He was wrong, Marcy thought. They couldn't go back. Things between them were changing too fast, too drastically. Nothing would be the same again.

7

PAUL'S BEDROOM was dominated by a huge four-poster, dimly illuminated by the glow of the table lamp.

For a moment Marcy was shaken with doubts about the wisdom of making love with Paul. She stared down, admiring the faded glory of the green-and-gold Aubusson carpet and tried to think. Two major issues were still unresolved: who Stephanie's mother really was and Paul's belief that she was that person. Did that affect how he saw her as a person? And if it did, was it negative or positive? She didn't know. She doubted that Paul did, either.

"Marcy?" Paul took her into his arms and pulled her against him.

She snuggled closer, resting her head on his damp sweater and breathing in its aroma of soap, marigolds and wet wool.

He dropped a kiss upon her tousled hair. "I want very much to make love to you, but if your fascination with the pattern in my carpet means that you're trying to decide how to tell me you've changed your mind, just say so. I can wait."

Marcy looked up, saw the tenderness in his dark eyes, and felt her heart contract with longing. What was it about this man that affected her so strongly? She didn't know. But if she didn't make love to him right now, she'd regret it for the rest of her life.

"Please don't wait," she said simply, and his arms tightened their grip, molding her to his body. His lips met hers with a rough hunger she found intoxicating. She opened her mouth and his tongue lightly stroked over hers, sending a torrent of sensation racing through her.

Paul raised his head and stared at her, a smile slowly tilting the corners of his lips, crinkling the skin around his eyes. "You, my sweet, have a large splotch of mud on your face. And on your left ear and—"

Marcy flicked away the bent flower petal that decorated his collar. "In other words, I look like you?"

He chuckled. "Probably. Why don't we take a shower?"

Marcy felt a swift stab of excitement. "I'm game." She tried to sound calmer than she felt at that moment.

Paul took her hand, guided her across his bedroom and through an open door.

She blinked in surprise. This bathroom was about as far removed from the utilitarian, white ceramic facility attached to her bedroom as it could be. The free-standing shower was constructed of a dark green, marblelike material with a faint vein of gold running through it. A huge square tub, fashioned of the same green substance and set with whirlpool jets, was tucked beneath a window. Along the opposite wall was a matching marble counter with twin sinks, decorated with stylized flowers baked in the enamel. Above the counter, the wall was mirrored to the ceiling. Deep green, black and gold metallic wallpaper in a paisley pattern covered the other three walls. Thick white-and-gold throw rugs were scattered around the green, black and white ceramic-tiled floor.

"This is fantastic! It looks like something out of a movie set!" Marcy exclaimed. Focusing on the decor gave her time to think. How was she to get from where she was to where she wanted to be—in the shower with Paul?

Paul glanced around as if seeing the room for the first time. "I guess it is rather effective. Margie, one of my firm's investment counselors, has a son who is studying architecture, and last year he needed to design a bath for a project. This one hadn't been touched since my parents were first married, so I let him have a go at it."

He reached into the shower and turned a faucet. Water began to spray out of the two rows of jets that ran up three sides of the stall.

"How nice," Marcy observed, then fell silent.

"Marcy," Paul said seriously, "does your chatter about my decorating mean that you feel as uncertain as I do?"

"You feel uncertain?" she asked in surprise.

"Damn right I do," he admitted. "I want to make love to you so badly, I'm shaking. But I want you to enjoy it as much as I do, and I'm not sure . . ."

It was strange, but just knowing that the normally very cool and competent Paul wasn't totally in control dispelled a great deal of Marcy's nervousness.

She laughed. "And you've already used up your spontaneous act for the night."

He grimaced. "Probably just as well, the way I feel at the moment."

"Darling Paul." Marcy hesitated no longer. Slipping her arms around his lean waist, she pressed herself against him. "I don't feel all that sure of myself, either," she told him.

Paul nuzzled the skin behind her ear and whispered, "How about if we form a mutual aid society? I'll help you, if you'll help me."

"Lovely," she murmured, then gasped when he picked her up and stepped into the shower.

She buried her face against his neck, feeling the roughness of his chin scrape across her forehead.

"Paul?"

"Yes, my sweet?"

"Why are we standing in the shower with our clothes on?" She pressed kisses along his jawline.

"I told you. Because we were rolling around in the mud."

"And the flowers," she added, watching a bright orange petal float across the green marble floor and disappear down the drain.

Paul chuckled. "True. Life is so unpredictable around you." Slowly he released her, letting her body slide the length of his.

Once her feet were on the floor, he stepped back and yanked his sweater over his head, then dropped the sodden garment onto the tile floor. It was going to be ruined, Marcy thought. She should pick it up. But before she could act, he grabbed the edge of her shirt and pulled it up over her head.

She squeaked in surprise, then gasped as he swiftly unfastened her bra and tossed it over the top of the shower stall. Suddenly feeling shy, her reserve dissolved beneath his gaze. He was staring at her as if she were the most beautiful thing he'd ever seen.

Reaching up, Marcy unbuttoned his shirt and pushed it off his shoulders, while water splashed over his chest, darkening his body hair to black. Curious now, she ran her fingers across the skin stretched taut over his shoulders, then pressed her palms flat against his chest and rubbed them in a circular motion. The heat coming from his body seemed warmer than the water that was all around them.

"Hmm," he groaned softly. "That feels so good."

Encouraged, Marcy stepped closer, pressing her breasts against him. A torrent of sensation twisted through her, fueling the intensity of her desire. She felt as if the very essence of herself was being melted and reshaped into something else.

"Marcy, I—" Paul was fumbling with the zipper on her jeans.

Eager by now, Marcy tugged the wet denim over her legs and kicked the jeans aside, while Paul disposed of his own pants.

He reached around behind her and turned off the water, but Marcy barely noticed. Her attention was focused on Paul, on the perfection of his body, on its overwhelming masculinity. She wanted to explore each and every inch of it, first with her eyes, then with her hands and finally with her lips. She wanted to savor all of it.

Paul didn't have as much patience. Scooping her into his arms, he hurried into the bedroom.

The cooler air barely registered on her wet body. She was far too caught up by the sensation of his bare skin against her own.

"My precious, precious Marcy." His husky voice made her feel cherished as she had never felt before and she found the experience incredibly erotic.

Paul gently laid her upon the bed, then stretched out beside her.

Marcy immediately wrapped her arms around him and pressed an eager kiss upon his lips, making no attempt to hide how she felt.

"Don't worry," he murmured. "I'll take care of everything." Propping himself on one elbow he fumbled in the drawer of the bedside table, finally pulling out a thin gold package. "I would never do anything to hurt you," he said.

Not intentionally, Marcy thought with a shiver of unease. But what about unintentionally? She was venturing into very deep emotional waters. What would be the consequences?

Then he slipped between her legs and lowered his body onto hers, and all her doubts dissolved in the feelings that tore through her as his hair-covered chest moved over the tips of her breasts. His weight pushed her deeper into the thick satin comforter, but she didn't feel confined. On the contrary, it was strangely liberating. She felt freer than she ever had before—free to explore all that being a woman entailed.

Paul cupped her face between his hands and met her lips in a scorching kiss. Slowly he pushed forward and penetrated her.

Marcy's breath was caught in her throat. She stared up; his eyes seemed to glow, lit by his desire for her.

She surged forward, intensifying the sensation that was spiraling through her almost beyond endurance.

"Slowly," he groaned. "I'm about to lose control."

"Good." Marcy began to nibble at his left shoulder, grazing the skin with her teeth. "It feels fantastic when you lose control."

Then he began to move, and Marcy pushed her forehead against his shoulder, focusing her attention inward. Finally, when she felt as if she couldn't stand it any longer, the cord of tension snapped, sending a wave through her that seemed to short-circuit her mind, suspending all rational thought.

Consciousness slowly returned, and she realized that Paul was lying over her limply, his breath coming in short, hard gasps.

A smile curved her lips as she idly ran her fingers over his sweat-slick spine. She felt omnipotent, a woman of infinite power, and wanted to hold on to the feeling. And to Paul.

MARCY HUNG ON to that feeling all through the following morning, a morning when she was unable to squeeze in even a moment alone with Paul. Stephanie clung to her like glue. Realizing the girl was nervous about the upcoming dance, Marcy stifled her own inclinations and concentrated on reassuring her.

Later, she promised herself as she listened to the sound of Paul's lawn mower. Stephanie was going to have her hair styled this afternoon, so she'd be alone with Paul for well over an hour. And anything could happen in an hour!

After lunch, Stephanie had barely left when Clementia called to ask Paul if he would mind driving her and several of her friends to a garden show in Malden, because the driver they'd originally asked had suddenly come down with the flu.

The disappointed expression on Paul's face as he talked to his aunt made Marcy feel a little better. That helped her to smile and assure him that she understood perfectly.

After all, she reminded herself, families tended to be like that. Whoever became involved with Paul was going to have to realize his family was very important to him. And there was always tonight, Marcy thought in anticipation. Aunt Clementia, tired out from her day of viewing the floral exhibits, would undoubtedly go to bed early. Stephanie would be at her dance. All Marcy had to do was bide her time.

That task grew harder and harder; the day crept by.

FINALLY, when Marcy was seriously thinking she'd been caught in a time warp, evening came.

Stephanie waltzed into the living room, her taffeta skirt rustling enticingly. "What do you think?"

Paul uttered an exaggerated wolf whistle and Marcy said, "Fantastic, absolutely fantastic. Wearing your hair off your face in a fall of curls is inspired. It makes you look like a Victorian debutante."

Stephanie blinked uncertainly. "It does? The hair-dresser said it's the newest style."

Marcy chuckled. "I have a historian friend who claims that fashion isn't new. It's cyclical. She says that if you just wait long enough, everything comes back."

"My lipstick isn't too light, is it?" Stephanie stuck out her lower lip and squinted down.

"Not a bit. You look absolutely perfect," Marcy assured her.

"Smile," Paul ordered, a fraction of a second before the flash went off.

"Uncle Paul, you're as bad as Mom. She always . . ." Stephanie gulped and her lower lip trembled.

"You miss your mother tonight," Marcy said, putting Stephanie's pain into words.

"Yeah. I wish she were here to see my dress. And she probably is," she ended in a rush.

"I think so, too," Paul agreed huskily. "What time is your ride picking you up?"

"Jessie's mom will be here in a minute."

"Jessie's mom?" Marcy asked curiously. "I thought you said Jessie's boyfriend was going to drive the four of you, since your date doesn't have his license yet?"

"He was, but he got a speeding ticket a couple days ago, and his father told him that he was never going to drive anything of his again except the riding mower and he hasn't relented yet. So Jessie's mom said she'd drive us since she was going to be there as a chaperon, anyway."

"Thank the powers that be for Jessie's mom," Marcy said. "She sounds like—"

A car horn sounded from the front of the house, and Stephanie took one last look at her reflection in the mirror above the breakfront.

"You look spectacular," Paul encouraged her. "Go have fun."

For a second, Stephanie looked bleak, then straightened her shoulders and gave them both a determined smile. "I will. Don't wait up for me. I have a key, remember?" She left on a wave of perfume.

Marcy turned and saw the bleakness reflected in Paul's face. She wanted to comfort him, to put her arms around him and hold him safe. But the simple fact that they had become lovers stopped her. She didn't want him to think she was reading more into their relationship than he was. She didn't know if making love with her last night had just been a spur-of-the-moment impulse.... But then, she reminded herself, Paul was not an impulsive man. Not really. He almost always acted for a reason, even if it wasn't apparent. Even his joking attempts at spontaneity had been for a reason.

Much as Stephanie had, Paul seemed to be making an effort to shake off his unhappy mood.

"Want to play chess?" she asked, trying to give his thoughts a new direction.

"Have you thought up a new way to cheat?" he scoffed.

Marcy sniffed. "I didn't cheat. I outwitted you. There's a difference."

"Not in the end result."

"All right, if you're going to hold a grudge, you pick the game."

"Well," he said slowly, "I haven't used up my day's spontaneous impulse yet."

"Oh?" Marcy heard her voice grow husky.

"We could play poker."

"I don't know how."

"All the better. Let's play strip poker."

Marcy laughed. "Are you trying to take advantage of me?"

"Yes," he said simply, "but only if you want me to."

"I want, I want." She took his hand and followed him upstairs, into a world that held only pleasure and promise—a world where no everyday problems could intrude—a world she desperately craved to enter, even if for only a short time.

BY THE NIGHT of the séance, Marcy was beginning to feel as if time were slipping through her fingers like so many grains of sand. Try as she might, she couldn't block out her problems. Who was Stephanie's mother? What could she do about her crumbling base of support in her quest for the chairmanship? And why was she finding it so difficult to concentrate on her book?

Maybe she ought to consult Clementia's crystal ball for a few answers, Marcy thought. She squinted at herself in the dresser mirror, trying to judge how thick her eyelashes looked. Undecided, she added a little more mascara and stepped back to study the overall effect.

Not bad. Not bad at all. She twisted sideways, and her black silk skirt swished sensuously around her legs. She adjusted the deeply scooped neckline of the matching silk top. Picking up a silver shawl with its intricate pattern of shining, iridescent leaves, she draped it across her shoulders.

"Marcy?" It was Stephanie.

"Come in."

Stephanie erupted into the room. "Wow!" Her eyes widened. "You look gorgeous. Like a Gypsy. All you need is a rose between your teeth."

Marcy laughed. "Thank you."

"What do you think of my outfit?" Stephanie twirled, sending the gauzy edges of her full skirt billowing out.

Marcy studied the way the thin white fabric seemed to float around the girl's slender figure.

"You look ethereal," she said at last. "Is that on purpose?"

Stephanie giggled. "Yeah. I thought this would be exactly right for a séance. Jessie loaned it to me. She wore it when she was Ophelia in the school play last year. It's from the scene where she drowns herself."

"Ah." Marcy nodded sagely. "That's it. You look like you've been in the water too long."

"Marcy! I'm serious. Dad always said you get more out of an experience if you project yourself into it."

"Well, if you project yourself any deeper, you'll get wet," Marcy said, pleased by the natural way Stephanie had referred to her father. "Why don't you go practice drifting down the stairs? It'll add to the illusion."

Stephanie beamed at her. "That's a great idea. I'll go show Mrs. Bailey what I look like. Maybe Morgan'll be there."

"Morgan?" Marcy tried to place the name but failed.

"Her son. He's a senior at MIT."

Marcy chuckled. "Ah, the lure of the older man."

"Not only that, but he's gorgeous." Stephanie heaved a sigh and left.

Marcy ran her fingers through her hair and, picking up her black evening purse, turned to follow. She jumped when Paul suddenly materialized in the doorway, catching her breath. Her eyes skimmed over the pristine whiteness of his dress shirt, the somber perfection of his striped tie and the sartorial splendor of his gray suit, to linger for a second on the breadth of his shoulders. Then her gaze was drawn upward to study his face.

She saw his eyes widen, too, as he took in her outfit, but unlike Stephanie's, they didn't linger on her shimmering shawl. They homed in on the swell of her breasts that was visible above the deeply cut neckline.

Marcy felt a surge of feminine power at the sight of the glow of desire that flared in his eyes. "Yes?" she said breathlessly.

Paul dragged his eyes from her décolletage, blinked and said, "I came to see what one wears to a séance."

"I don't know about one, but Stephanie is going as the ghost of Ophelia."

"And you intend to seduce the spirits back into the world?" he said huskily.

"Mmm." Marcy savored his impression of her as a seductress. Usually people saw her intelligence first, her competitiveness second, while her femininity came in a distant third.

"What you're wearing looks exactly right," she finally said. "Very dignified."

"For what promises to be a very undignified event. Shall we go?" He held out his hand and Marcy unhesitatingly took it. A shiver chased over her at the feel of his warm fingers. Suddenly the night seemed alive with possibilities.

They found Clementia waiting in the living room of her cottage. Her thin cheeks were flushed with excitement, and anticipation lent a happy sparkle to her faded blue eyes.

"Ah, my dears. Come in. Come in. Madame Zola hasn't arrived yet. I can't tell you how excited I am."

Paul smiled indulgently. "You look it."

"My garden club can hardly wait for my report tomorrow. I told them all about how you'd arranged a séance for my birthday. They're all so thrilled. Not one of them has ever gotten a present even vaguely like it." She smiled in satisfaction. "Margot told her husband that's what she wants, so he's going to call you this week to find out the particulars."

"Lovely," Paul muttered. "Not only do I advise him how to handle his investments, but now I'm supposed to tell him how to handle the spirit world."

"At least he doesn't know you had your palm read," Marcy whispered.

"Palm read?" Clementia had clearly overheard.

"Mmm, I was thinking of getting my palm read for my birthday," Marcy improvised at the sight of Paul's apprehensive expression.

"Tea leaves are more reliable, dear. Don't worry. You'll soon get the knack of it," Clementia said.

"Getting your palm read isn't much of a birthday present," Stephanie added doubtfully. "Especially not when you're going to be thirty-five."

"Thirty-five is young," Clementia scoffed.

"Not that young," Stephanie insisted. "Marcy's old enough to be my mother."

"I am not your mother," Marcy replied automatically.

"I need a drink." Paul headed toward the liquor cabinet. He was probably going to need several drinks before the evening was over, he thought. What with the séance, the fact that by now probably everyone who'd ever known him was aware he'd arranged this trip to the spirit world, Stephanie's insistence on claiming Marcy as her mother, Marcy's refusal to admit it—and that damned dress Marcy was wearing... He poured a generous measure of whiskey into a tumbler and took a long swallow.

All he really wanted to do was take her into his arms and kiss her. To feel her soft lips pressed against his. To savor the tremors of her muscles as her body quivered. He felt a surge of heat engulf his face and extend to the very tips of his ears.

He polished off the whiskey and poured some more. But it wasn't just the fantastic sex. There was a whole lot more to his feelings for Marcy than that. Take her personality. She was the most vital person he'd ever met. She seemed to find enjoyment in everything around her. She radiated a quicksilver happiness that drew him like the proverbial moth to the flame. He took another gulp of whiskey.

"What do you think, Paul?" he heard his aunt ask, and he turned to the women.

"Well?" Clementia repeated.

"Well, what?" He recalled himself with an effort.

"Round or square?" Stephanie prompted him.

His eyes instinctively went to Marcy's neckline. "Definitely round," he muttered.

"I told you," Clementia crowed. "Everyone knows you use a round table when you're summoning the spirits."

"Spirits?" Paul repeated blankly; he caught sight of Marcy's laughing brown eyes.

Poor man, she thought. Wherever his mind had been, it certainly hadn't been on tables. Was he really that concerned about what his friends thought? Probably not. If it really had been that important to him, he'd never have become involved in the whole thing to start with. He was probably just tired. He certainly hadn't gotten much sleep last night. She gave him an understanding smile, then frowned when his eyes developed a fixed, glazed expression.

He really was tired. What he needed was an early night. Another question popped unbidden into her mind. How did he normally sleep? In pajamas? Maybe just the bottoms? In the nude? A heavy weight settled on her chest.

"...enough?"

Marcy caught only the last word of Clementia's question. "Definitely," she muttered. Paul in the nude was enough for any woman.

"Good," Clementia continued, plainly oblivious to the fact that Marcy didn't have the vaguest idea what was being said. "I asked Mrs. Bailey to come too, but she didn't want to. She did say, though, that if we ever get a vampire, she'd be here with bells on."

"She'd do better to wear garlic," Paul said. "I know I'm going to be sorry I asked, but why would my housekeeper want to meet a vampire?"

"You *are* kidding?" Stephanie stared at him in shock.

"Believe me, a housekeeper who likes vampires is not my idea of a joking matter."

"Vampires are romantic," Marcy explained.

"Even I know that," Clementia threw in her two cents' worth.

"Romantic!" Paul stared at them, suspecting he was being made the butt of a joke. Three pairs of earnest eyes stared back at him.

"Really," Marcy elaborated. "If you don't believe us, read one of Anne Rice's books."

"Or watch 'Dark Shadows.'" Stephanie shivered in delight.

To Paul's relief, the doorbell rang, and Clementia rushed to answer it, trailed by the eager Stephanie and a curious Marcy.

"I have arrived," Madame Zola announced in ringing tones and strode into the room, followed by a wispy-looking woman somewhere in her forties.

"I'm so glad you could come," Clementia said.

Madame Zola ignored her as she took stock of the cozy living room. Finally she nodded. "Not perfect, but it will do."

"I like it," Clementia pointed out. "I find English country very restful."

Madame Zola fixed her with a reproving eye. "I do not refer to the furniture, but to the atmosphere. I must have a suitable atmosphere to be able to communicate with the great beyond."

"Wow!" Stephanie gasped, clearly impressed.

Paul shook his head at the gullibility of youth and took another sip of whiskey.

"Ah, very good!" Madame Zola nodded approvingly. "The unbeliever is drinking." She walked toward the round table Clementia had had moved to the middle of the room.

"I have not been drinking!" Paul put his glass down with a thump. "And who, may I ask, is your friend?"

"I didn't know how many of you there would be." Madame Zola's sharp eyes swept over the four of them.

"Meaning?" Paul asked.

"Numerology is important in contacting the spirit world. We must have an uneven number of supplicants at the table to complete the circle. If there had not been enough of you, then my dear cousin Ursula would have obliged us."

And if we'd had an even number, the response would have been the same, Paul thought cynically. Was Ursula there to help with the séance, or was she there to see what she could steal while their attention was focused elsewhere?

"We invited the housekeeper, but she only likes vampires," Clementia confided.

"Can you produce a vampire?" Stephanie asked eagerly.

"If I find a vampire, I keep him," Madame Zola pronounced. "The TV I also watch."

Paul shook his head in disbelief. "I think you're all nuts."

"He's a good boy, but he tends to be a little too literal," Clementia whispered to Madame Zola.

"I know." Madame Zola's shrug was a masterpiece of resignation.

"Can we get started?" Stephanie bounced in her chair with eagerness.

"If that is your wish?" Madame Zola glanced at Marcy, who nodded in agreement.

"Then if you will all please be seated." Madame Zola gestured toward the table. "Cousin Ursula shall stand at my left shoulder."

Once Madame Zola had them arranged around the table to her liking, she majestically lowered her gaunt body into the last empty chair. Ursula stood behind her, looking for all the world like a crow.

"There must be silence." Madame Zola frowned at Stephanie, who was whispering to Clementia.

"Now then, you will all join hands to form a circle," she continued. "I must caution you that if you break the circle for any reason, the séance will be ended. It is only your combined will, coupled with my gift, that will draw the spirits to us."

Marcy obediently took Clementia's paper-thin hand in her left and Paul's in her right. She felt the calluses on his palm, then the warmth of his skin seeped into hers. It made her feel excited and safe all at once.

"Ursula. The ball!" Madame Zola commanded.

Ursula took a large crystal ball attached to a thick mahogany base from the bag she was carrying and set it in front of Madame Zola.

"How lovely!" Clementia exclaimed. "May I touch it?"

"Certainly not!" Madame Zola snapped. "It is a thing of power. My power."

"Sorry," Clementia said meekly, while Marcy studied the ball. What was there about it that Madame Zola was afraid Clementia might discover if she examined it at close range?

"You must all close your eyes," Madame Zola intoned.

Marcy mentally applauded the woman's soothing, rhythmic cadence. Madame Zola would make a fantastic hypnotist. She—

Marcy's train of thought was suddenly derailed when she felt Paul's foot rubbing over her calf. The abrasiveness of his sock sent a shiver through her. Up and down, back and forth his foot moved, heating the skin on her calf to an intolerable level. Of all the times for him to indulge in sexual teasing, she thought in a confusing mixture of exasperation and longing.

Marcy tried to inch away from him, but was stymied when Madame Zola hissed disapprovingly.

The movement finally stopped, but before Marcy had time to regain her equilibrium, Paul's fingers began to rub over the sensitive skin of her inner wrist. Marcy tensed her muscles in an attempt to control her reaction, but it didn't work. Her nerves felt stretched to the breaking point and her mouth was dry as dust.

Blast Paul and whatever game he was playing! She glared at his profile and received a gleaming smile in return. This bordered on sadism. Just wait until she got him alone! She'd deal with him the way he deserved to be dealt with. Her heartbeat seemed to stop, then go into overdrive as a whole assortment of possibilities bubbled through her mind, driven by the force of desire.

A startled squeak from Stephanie reminded Marcy of why they were holding hands in the first place, and she looked up. She felt her eyes widen as the crystal ball began to glow with an unearthly yellow light.

Fascinated, Marcy watched the glow intensify, taking on a greenish hue. As she stared, an image seemed to form. It gathered substance from the misty tendrils of light until at last a distinct set of features was visible.

Marcy swallowed uneasily, tightening her grip on Paul's hand. Even though she knew that what she was seeing was simply high tech applied to fortune-telling, she still found it unnerving.

"Yes, I can hear you." Madame Zola's eerie voice raised goose bumps on Marcy's bare arms.

"It's Caleb Wycoff!" Clementia gasped. For a second the image wavered, then grew stronger.

"Silence!" Madame Zola warned. "I must have silence to hear. He says . . ." She paused, as if listening, then said, "He says he has been wronged."

"I knew it!" Clementia exclaimed. "I told you he couldn't be as bad as everyone painted him."

"He was worse," Paul muttered.

"Do not anger the spirit, oh unbeliever," Madame Zola chided. "My hold on him is very tenuous."

Marcy glanced at Ursula. She had moved slightly behind Madame Zola and to one side, but Marcy couldn't tell if she was the one responsible for creating the effect. She looked at Stephanie, who was watching the crystal ball with the wide-eyed wonder teenagers usually reserved for pop stars.

"He says that he did not kill his second wife. She tripped on the parapet and fell to her death."

"What about the first one?" Paul asked dryly.

The image seemed to glow brighter for a second.

"He says she was a nag," Madame Zola explained simply.

"I can see where that might drive a man to murder," Paul agreed.

"Lots of things can drive a person to murder!" Marcy whispered and hastily moved her leg out of reach as his foot started wandering again.

"He says that he is very annoyed with his descendant," Madame Zola intoned.

"Me?" Stephanie squeaked fearfully.

"No. His male descendant."

All five women turned and stared at Paul.

"He says that it displeases him that he has not married and produced sons to carry on the name. He says that the time is right and the signs are favorable to do so."

Blast it all, anyway, Marcy thought in exasperation. She felt Paul's body begin to shake with suppressed laughter. Madame Zola obviously thought that she was doing her a favor, but all she was doing was providing Paul with a great deal of amusement. If he should think that she'd put Madame Zola up to it... Her skin crawled at the thought.

"Caleb Wycoff says that his descendant must have sons. Many sons. And daughters," Madame Zola added at Stephanie's disgruntled mutter. The ball began to flicker and the image faded.

"He's gone." Stephanie sounded disappointed.

"But it was wonderful while he was here." Clementia sighed happily. "That was the very best birthday present I ever had. Thank you, my dears. And you too, Madame Zola."

"I am glad to have been able to be of some small service," Madame Zola said faintly, while her assistant hurriedly bundled the crystal ball into the sack.

Regretfully, Marcy watched it disappear. She'd have liked to have found out how it worked. She already knew how effective it was. Even supposing that Madame Zola was a fraud, she'd still been impressed by the act, although she could have done without the little plug for matrimony.

Marcy glanced at Paul and found him watching her. Her eyes dropped to their linked hands and she hastily pulled away.

He grinned at her boyishly and she found herself grinning back. Life suddenly seemed to hold all kinds of exciting options.

8

HEMLINES, Marcy wrote across the top of the blank sheet of paper, then stared down, seeking inspiration. None came. Despite the businesslike atmosphere of Paul's study and the luxury of a quiet, empty house, she couldn't seem to concentrate.

She drew a happy face in the margin and added Paul's dimple to it.

"Stop wasting time," she told herself. "You're supposed to be working for another..." She glanced at the clock on the mantel. It read two-thirty. "Another two hours, minimum."

She sighed. The simple fact was that she didn't care about hemlines. Or clothes. But she should. She had a contract to produce a detailed outline of this book by December. The thought of December reminded her that she had another deadline, too. Finding Stephanie's mother, so that she, Marcy Handley, could become chair of the Psychology Department.

She eyed the phone sitting on Paul's desk. Maybe Daniel had something to report about the handwriting comparisons. If he'd kept to his original schedule, he'd have been back from his conference for a few days. And even if he hadn't finished the analysis yet, her call might hurry him along.

Marcy picked up the phone and punched his number in.

Daniel answered on the second ring.

"Hi, Daniel. This is Marcy. Have you had a chance to get to those signatures yet?"

"I finished last night. I was going to give you a call this evening."

"And?" Marcy prodded, impatient now. "Did any of the signatures match?"

"Yes, the signature on the photostat you sent matches the one of the person who signed herself, 'Your loving niece, Linda.'"

"Linda! You're sure?"

"Damn right I'm sure! It's my job to be sure, but if you'd like a second opinion . . ." His voice trailed away into offended silence.

"Don't you dare go all temperamental on me, Daniel. I'm just surprised, that's all."

Shocked would be more like it. Linda must have been barely sixteen when Stephanie was born. Not only that, but from what she remembered, Linda had been a very reserved teenager. Her parents had kept her sheltered, both from other kids and life in general. Marcy couldn't even remember her dating, let alone having a steady boyfriend. In fact, Marcy's mother had always claimed that Linda's parents' strictness was the reason the girl had opted to live with her grandmother when she turned sixteen.

"Please, don't say a word about this to anyone yet," Marcy said. "I want to talk to Linda before I tell anyone."

"It's none of my business," Daniel assured her. "Give me a call when you get back to town, and you can repay me by buying me dinner."

"My pleasure. Thanks again, Daniel."

She hung up, swiveled around in her chair and stared blindly out the window, trying to arrange what she remembered to fit what Daniel had just told her.

First she recalled what her mother had said about her grandmother being uneasy talking about the past. Could she have known about Linda's child?

Somehow that didn't ring true. Her grandmother had a rigid code of morality as well as a bone-deep sense of family. She would never have been a party to sending her first great-grandchild out of the family. Not when she must have known that at least two of her children would have gladly adopted the baby—Marcy's own parents included.

No, her grandmother couldn't have known. Linda must have had Stephanie before she'd gone to live with her grandmother, which meant that she'd had help during her pregnancy. Linda couldn't have been living at home during that time, or the whole family would have known that she was expecting. And there would have been medical bills and living expenses. So who had helped? Linda's parents? But if that were the case, why had she assumed her cousin's identity?

Marcy sighed in frustration. The only person who could answer those questions was Linda herself, and she was now living in Manhattan. But whatever Linda's explanation proved to be, now Marcy knew the truth. Now she could clear her name. Now there was nothing standing between her and the position she had worked so hard for.

So why wasn't she more elated? She should be. Now she could tell Stephanie who really was her biological mother. And after all, she'd come a long way toward helping the girl deal with her feelings of grief and begin to make friends with her uncle. In fact, she had accomplished everything she'd set out to do. Even Paul's intriguing suggestion that she give a workshop for his female employees wasn't really a valid excuse to stay on. She could always return for it. So why did the thought of leaving give her a sick feeling in the pit of her stomach?

Because she was madly in love with Paul Wycoff. She immediately tried to deny it. She couldn't be. She just couldn't. She didn't even want to be. It simply wouldn't work. Paul lived in Boston and her life revolved around her job in Indiana. How could a relationship thrive in those circumstances? All they'd have would be flying weekend visits every month or so, and in between times, she'd be sitting around her empty apartment, remembering his lovemaking and fantasizing about the next time they could be together.

Marcy flung her pencil onto the desktop and walked to the window. She pushed aside the sheer draperies and stared into the peaceful backyard. All she could see was a cardinal flittering through the bushes and a small white dog unsuccessfully trying to stalk a robin. Farther back, Clementia's dense moat of marigolds nodded gently in the breeze, and Marcy could see the bees hovering above the blossoms. It was simply peaceful, far removed from the stresses of modern life. Somehow absolutely right, the perfect setting in which to recharge one's batteries after a trying day of competing in the outside world.

Everything about Paul's home was perfect, including its inhabitants. Stephanie was a dear and Clementia... Marcy smiled. Clementia was a darling who brought an enthusiasm to life that few twenty-year-olds possessed, let alone octogenarians. And Paul...Marcy sighed longingly.

She turned from the window and wandered to the sofa, sinking into its soft down cushions. Paul was exactly right, too. Not perfect. In fact, he was far different from her image of the ideal man.

But when it came to the important things like loyalty and character and honesty, Paul had them all. In abundance. When the chips were down, he could be counted on. He was a man for the long haul, not just for short-term pleasure.

He was, as her grandmother was fond of saying, the stuff of which great husbands could be fashioned. Nonetheless, Marcy faced reality squarely. Not only had he not asked her to marry him, but she wasn't even sure she wanted him to. If he didn't ask her, then she wouldn't have to make a choice between him and the job she'd coveted for so long.

"Oh, Marcy, you've really done it this time," she muttered. "The question is, where do you go from here?"

"Heartbreak Hotel"? The old song title popped into her mind. It could well come to that, she thought grimly. But not without a fight. What she needed to do was decide what she *really* wanted out of life.

But how did *he* feel about *her*? She leaned her head against the back of the sofa and stared at the ceiling, trying to use her skills as a counselor to assess his actions, beginning to tick off points she thought were facts and not just wishful thinking.

He enjoyed her company. He really enjoyed making love with her. Some things a man could fake, but that wasn't one of them. Sexually they were an explosive combination, and as far as she could assess his reactions, he was as aware of it as she was. He also respected her intelligence, was interested in her research and valued her opinion. And he'd never tried to downgrade the importance of her career.

But their relationship hadn't been all positive. He still didn't believe her claim that Stephanie wasn't her daughter, though he didn't appear to blame her for what he seemed to feel had been a youthful indiscretion. In fact, his conviction that she was Stephanie's mother had been more positive than negative up to this point. But could his feelings for her be colored by the fact that he wanted Stephanie to be happy?

So what should she do now? Marcy stared at the phone for a long moment before deciding against calling her cousin. She wanted to see Linda's face when she confronted her with what she knew. There was also the possibility of someone overhearing a phone conversation. Someone such as Linda's husband. Marcy tried to remember what she knew about Edward. It wasn't much. She'd only met him once, seven years ago, at their wedding, and presumably his mind had been on other things than talking to his bride's cousin.

Her mind suddenly made up, she pulled the phone book out of the middle desk drawer and looked up the number of the airline's reservation desk. Ten minutes later she was booked on a flight leaving Boston at seven in the morning, in two days' time. After all, she'd promised to drive Clementia and two of her elderly friends to a flower show in the suburbs, or so she justified the delay to herself.

The plain truth was, however, that she wanted to spend just one more day with Paul.

MARCY DIDN'T WANT to cast a shadow on their enjoyment of Stephanie's band concert at school that evening, so she put off mentioning her travel plans until breakfast the following morning.

"By the way..." She tried to sound casual as she handed Paul a cup of steaming coffee. "I have to fly down to New York City tomorrow morning for a day."

"No!" Stephanie's violent reaction took her by surprise. "You can't go! You're my mother!"

"Stephanie, I'm only staying overnight," Marcy said soothingly, wondering why she was so upset. Even given the violent upheavals in her life these last months, an overnight business trip wasn't really that big a deal. Was Stephanie afraid she wouldn't come back?

Paul watched the expressions flit across Marcy's face. *Would* she be back? He still didn't know for certain why she'd agreed to come to Boston in the first place, so he couldn't be sure she didn't feel that she'd accomplished her purpose and was using the pretext of a trip to New York as a way of making a graceful exit. And why had she had to pick this morning, of all mornings, to drop her bombshell? When he already felt like . . . He blocked the thought, forcing himself to focus on the problem at hand.

He didn't want her to go because he loved her. He finally confronted the knowledge that had been nagging at him for days. He loved her calm competence, her intelligence, her compassion, her independence and the enthusiasm she brought to life. He felt alive around her. It no longer even bothered him that Stephanie liked her so much. How could it? He, too, thought Marcy was something far out of the ordinary.

"But you're my mother!" Stephanie wailed again.

"Even mothers get time off for good behavior," Paul said, trying to lighten the atmosphere. He could understand Stephanie's desire to keep Marcy close. He felt that way himself, but had enough experience to know that trying to pressure someone by exerting emotional blackmail was a very bad idea. "I'm sure Marcy wouldn't be going to New York if it weren't important." He paused expectantly.

Marcy scrambled for an excuse that sounded plausible. "I need to discuss a couple aspects of my book with my editor," she said hastily.

Paul grew even more uneasy. He didn't know anything about publishing, but had plenty of common sense. Why would she fly all the way to New York City to talk to an editor when she could pick up the phone and do it? Even if Marcy wanted to show the editor something, he had a fax machine in the study that he'd given her permission to use.

But if she wasn't going to New York to talk to her editor, what was she planning to do there that she didn't want him to know about? His gaze narrowed and drifted over the soft contours of her lips as his mind began to replay the feel of them beneath his own.

He shifted in his seat, feeling his body began to react to the stimulus and stared blindly into his cup of coffee as he struggled to regain control. He'd always prided himself on being able to control all his appetites. But with Marcy... He crumbled a piece of toast onto his plate. With Marcy his body made demands that had no basis in rational thought. All he wanted to do was to make love to her. To pull her into his arms and drown in her sensual sweetness.

Paul looked up from the mess he was making of his breakfast and watched Marcy talking to Stephanie. The words rolled meaninglessly over his head as he concentrated on the movement of her fingers as she gestured to make a point.

Why did she want to go to New York City? And why now? The whole situation didn't add up, and he hated equations that didn't balance. A vital piece of information was missing, but he had no idea what it could be.

What was more, he'd never find out if she left. Unless... Unless he were to go with her. Excitement slammed through him at the idea. Not only would he find out what was going on, but they would be together for a whole day and night.

And if he went along, he could make sure she came back.

"But I still don't see why you need to see your editor," Stephanie was complaining. "Aren't I more important than some dumb old editor?"

"To me you are," Marcy said soothingly. "But it isn't a question of choosing. I have plenty of time in my life for both of you." *How I wish that were still true!* she thought miserably.

"It's simply a short business trip, Stephanie," Paul added encouragingly. "In fact, I've been meaning to get down to New York myself for weeks now to talk to a couple of financial analysts about investment opportunities in Eastern Europe. I think I'll go with you. That is, if you don't mind?" Paul held his breath and waited.

Marcy stared at him, a confusing mixture of feelings tumbling through her mind. The very thought of spending a whole day, to say nothing of a whole night, alone with Paul was intoxicating. But overshadowing the excitement was worry. What would be his reaction to her news about Linda? Would his feelings toward her change? Maybe she could tell him about Linda after they got back to Boston?

"Of course you can come," she said at last.

"And Stephanie can stay with Aunt Clementia while we're gone," Paul suggested.

"When are you leaving?" Stephanie asked.

"I have a seat on the seven o'clock shuttle tomorrow morning. If that's all right with you?" Marcy looked at Paul, hoping her intense anticipation wasn't visible.

"Sure." Paul ruthlessly jettisoned a full schedule of appointments. "Is that okay with you, Stephanie?"

"Why not?" Stephanie muttered.

"If something's bothering you, say so," Paul said, trying to use Marcy's method.

"What do you care if something's bothering me?" Stephanie glared, first at him then at Marcy. "You're helping *her* leave, and you never even remembered that . . ." Her lower lip began to tremble uncontrollably.

Paul stared into the depths of his coffee for a few minutes, then said roughly, "If you mean the date, of course I remembered. I never forgot. That's why I went for a walk at two o'clock last night, because I couldn't forget."

"Then why didn't you say something?" Stephanie cried. "You never said a word. Not one word. It was like I was the only one who remembered that today was

Mom's birthday. Like I was the only one who even remembered that she'd ever been alive at all. Like I was the only one who cared!"

"The only one..." Paul stared at her. "My God, Stephanie, do you have any idea how much I loved Hillary? She meant the world to me. She was more like a second mother to me than a sister. Nothing will ever be quite the same now that she's dead, and I'm finding it harder than hell to come to terms with it. Sometimes at night—" His voice cracked. He swallowed and forced himself to continue. "Sometimes at night I wake up in a cold sweat and I can't believe she's really gone. That I'll never see her again. Never hear that funny little laugh she had. Never threaten to do fiscally irresponsible things to her trust fund if she didn't quit dragging home all those friends of hers who she just knew would make me a perfect wife. Sometimes at work, when I'm thinking about other things, I pick up the phone to call her and tell her something and I suddenly remember that she's not at the other end of any phone line. And for you to say that I don't care..."

"I didn't know you felt like that," Stephanie mumbled. "How could I? You seemed to be going on like nothing had ever happened, except that I'd come to live with you."

Paul grimaced. "What did you expect me to do? Sit on the front steps and cry? Hell, I've felt like it time and time again, but you had enough to deal with without taking on my pain, too. I didn't want to make a miserable situation any worse for you."

"Nothing is worse than thinking you're all alone!" Stephanie cried. "Oh, Uncle Paul, I miss her so much." She threw herself at him.

Paul's arms tightened around her, gathering her close. He rocked back and forth while she sobbed as if her heart would break. "I know, Stephanie, I know."

Finally Stephanie raised her head, sniffed, hiccuped and said, "I'm sorry. I got your shirt all wet."

"I've got lots of shirts." Paul dropped a kiss on her head and let her go. "But I've only got one niece." He surreptitiously rubbed his eyes.

Stephanie had no such inhibitions. She scrubbed her wet face with the back of one hand and muttered, "I hate it when I cry. I look like a boiled fish. It's weird, Uncle Paul, but I feel much better now. I mean—" she gestured vaguely "—nothing's changed, but . . ."

"There's a lot of truth to the old adage that a trouble shared is a trouble halved," Marcy said.

"Stephanie..." Paul said slowly, "later I intend to go out and put flowers on Hillary's grave. Would you like to come with me?"

"It's a school day. . . ." Stephanie said hesitantly.

"This is far more important," he replied.

"I'd like to come," she told him. "And could we stop by the old North Church? Mom always said she felt like she was a part of history whenever she stood in it. Like she was part of a long line of people who'd lived and worshiped and . . . died there."

"Certainly." Paul nodded in understanding. "And Harvard." He unexpectedly chuckled. "Hillary wanted

to go to Harvard so badly, but it was an all-male school
back then, so every time we'd drive by, she'd lean out
the window and make a rude noise and an even ruder
comment about their sexism. And when your grandfather complained once, your grandmother said that
the Wycoffs had always been radicals, right back to the
one who'd helped dump the tea into Boston Harbor and
that, anyway, Hillary was right. They were a pack of
sexists."

"Really?" Stephanie's eyes lit up. "I didn't know that.
She never told me."

"She was probably afraid you'd turn into a radical,
too. Strange how much more conservative she became
as she got older." He turned to Marcy. "Would you like
to come with us?"

"No." Marcy refused, even though she really would
have liked to spend the time with him and Stephanie.
This was a pilgrimage the two of them needed to make
on their own.

"You really are welcome," Stephanie assured her.

"Thank you, but I have a few phone calls I need to
make, and I promised Clementia I'd drive her to a garden show in the city."

"My offer of the Mercedes still stands," Paul said,
then, steeling himself, he added, "I'll even show you
how to use a stick shift."

"No, thanks. I could never stand the suspense, wondering exactly when one of those homicidal maniacs
masquerading as commuters would hit me."

"None of them's ever hit me," Paul pointed out.

"Then you're overdue, and I don't want to be behind the wheel of that car when the law of averages catches up with you," Marcy said emphatically. "Clementia's friend has a nice little compact that's just my speed."

"When I get my driver's license in the spring, I'm going to drive the Mercedes," Stephanie announced.

"In your dreams," Paul said. "You ever even look at my Mercedes and I'll personally burn your license."

"But you were going to let Marcy drive it," Stephanie objected.

"That's different," Paul told her calmly.

"I don't see why. Exactly how is it different, Uncle Paul?" Her eyes gleamed with interest.

"Didn't anyone ever tell you that curiosity killed the cat?" Paul didn't have an answer for her. He might know exactly how he felt about Marcy, but had doubts about her feelings for him. All he knew was she didn't trust him enough to tell him what had happened all those years ago. The knowledge nagged at him like a sore tooth.

"People who mind their own business never find out anything," Stephanie said.

"Console yourself with the knowledge that they live longer."

"In ignorance," Stephanie said virtuously. "According to my teachers, ignorance is a state to be avoided at all costs."

"Personally, I've always liked the old saying about ignorance being bliss," Paul said.

Stephanie giggled. "Will you put that in writing so I can take it to geometry class?"

"Your teacher undoubtedly knows far more about ignorance than you or I ever will. Why don't you go ask your aunt if you can stay with her while we're in New York tomorrow?"

Marcy waited until Stephanie had left, then looked at Paul in mock wonder. "I'm really impressed," she said, deliberately keeping her tone light.

"Oh?" Paul looked skeptical. "Why?"

"I didn't think you'd be brave enough to tough that one out."

"There's lots of things you don't know about me." He gave her a wicked grin that made her want to begin exploring the subject at once.

"Maybe I should consult Madame Zola?"

"Only if they pay college professors in Indiana a damn sight better than they do here in Massachusetts."

"A good point." Marcy winced as she remembered the cost of the séance. "And to make matters worse, I'm not having much luck learning to read the tea leaves."

"You aren't?" He eyed her with fascination. The unexpected facets of her personality were what he loved most about Marcy. It was like traveling a winding road and finding a thing of priceless beauty while rounding a curve.

"Nope." Marcy sighed. "Clementia says that you either have the gift or you don't, and it appears I don't.

When I look into the bottom of the teacup all I see are wet leaves. Maybe I ought to switch to the tarot cards."

"Maybe you ought to admit you can't tell the future and be done with it," Paul suggested.

"Then there's always phrenology." She got to her feet and walked toward him, giving him a smile that raised his blood pressure fifty points.

"All right, I'll play straight man. What's phrenology?" He looked up, savoring the way her eyes were beginning to gleam with laughter. He found her laughter almost as seductive as her body.

Marcy leaned closer and threaded her fingers through his dark hair. It felt silky and warm. She flexed her fingers and gently rubbed his scalp. A very faint fragrance rose from his hair to tease her senses. It reminded her of the outdoors in the fall. Of crisp leaves, crisper nights and blazing fires. Of Paul and herself . . . She began to trace the outline of his ear.

"What are you doing?" His voice had deepened perceptibly.

"Phrenology. You can tell all about a person by feeling their lumps and protuberances."

"Now that's a concept that has some interesting ramifications." His voice was husky now.

"Protuberances on the head," she said tartly.

"Let me guess. You learned about it in Psychology 101?"

"No, from a friend of mine who's a gold mine of historical trivia."

"There's nothing the least bit trivial about this particular bit of information," he said. "This one could drive a man to distraction." Giving in to the urge to touch her, Paul turned slightly, grabbed her around the waist and pulled her over the back of the sofa.

"What are you doing?" Marcy demanded.

"This is what you said you wanted," he murmured as he positioned her across his lap and pulled her closer.

"It is?"

"You told me to try being more spontaneous."

"Well, yes, but . . ."

"Normally," he continued in a conversational tone, pushing back the hair from her forehead in a curiously intimate gesture, "when an attractive women starts running her fingers through my hair, I restrain the impulse to grab her and kiss her senseless."

"But?" Marcy whispered as he cupped her chin in his hard hand.

"But since I haven't used my spontaneous gesture for the day, this time I'm not going to."

"Lucky me." Marcy snuggled closer.

"Lucky both of us," he murmured and closed his mouth over hers.

She reached up and traced his outer ear with the tip of one forefinger. His skin felt cool, and her finger wandered lower, along his jawline. She found the difference in skin texture intriguing. Her fingernail rasped over his emerging beard, and the sensation raced right to her nerve endings.

Paul shuddered and gathered her still closer, kissing her with a need that she found far more appealing than the most practiced technique. It was as if he were driven by the same hunger that was consuming her.

"ARE YOU KISSING Marcy?" Stephanie's question jerked Marcy out of the haze of sexual euphoria that surrounded her.

Paul slowly raised his head, as if reluctant to break contact with Marcy's lips, and muttered, "One of us is going to have to have a talk with her, if she can't tell a kiss when she sees one."

"Oh, I know all about sex," Stephanie assured him. "Mom told me. She said that since most teenage boys don't think beyond the urgency of the moment, we girls have to. Actually—" she stared at him "—my question was . . . was more rhetorical. I was just kinda surprised."

"Kinda?" Now Marcy's curiosity got the better of her.

"Uh-huh. I noticed just the other night that lately, when you and Uncle Paul look at each other, it's kind of . . . like . . . different," she finished weakly. "Kinda like the two of you know a secret that no one else does. Do you?" She glanced eagerly from Paul to Marcy.

A secret? Marcy considered Stephanie's choice of words. Such as what?

"But if we had a secret and we told you, it wouldn't be a secret anymore, would it?" Paul reasoned.

Disappointed by his response, even though she wasn't sure why, Marcy tried to slide casually off his lap. It wasn't easy. She was as uncertain of her own feelings—and of Paul's—as if she'd been Stephanie's age.

9

"HERE, let me have that." Paul took Marcy's overnight case as they emerged from the tunnel into the airport terminal.

"I've made reservations for us at the Wilton. It's not far from either the consultant I want to talk to or your publisher's offices."

Marcy's thoughts had been on her visit with Linda; now she turned to Paul, trying to concentrate on what he was saying. She watched his lips move, but instead of hearing words, she was remembering how those lips had felt, pressed against her own. Remembering the slight scratchiness of his cheek and the fresh fragrance of the cologne he wore.

"Marcy?" Concern sharpened Paul's voice. "Are you ill?"

"Sorry." She made an effort to respond normally. "I'm just a little frazzled. I hate flying," she added truthfully.

He chuckled. "You don't have to tell me that. You bring a whole new meaning to the term 'white-knuckle flyer.' I was telling you that I made reservations at a hotel near your editor."

"Editor?" Marcy repeated blankly. "Oh, yes, of course." There was a lot more to lying than appeared on the surface, she thought ruefully. Morality aside, it required an excellent memory, better than the one she possessed.

"I think I'll see her this morning and get it out of the way," she said when Paul stopped at the curb beside the stand of taxis. "Why don't you check us into the hotel and I'll meet you back there when I've finished?" She held her breath, willing him to agree. She wanted to get the confrontation with Linda over and done with. It wasn't going to be a pleasant experience, for either for them, but it had to be faced.

"Fine, my appointment with the consultant isn't until later this afternoon." He nodded at the cabbie. "I'll drop you off at your publisher's offices. It's right on the way."

"Thank you." Marcy stifled a sigh; her inventive skills just weren't equal to the challenge of coming up with another on-the-spot lie.

Soon, she told herself encouragingly as she climbed into the back of the dusty taxi. Soon she could be totally open with Paul. But what would be the result of that openness? She felt a sudden lurch of fear, which she determinedly put out of her mind. *Worry about one thing at a time,* she told herself. *First Linda, then Paul.*

Marcy's nerves were already stretched to the breaking point, so the ride into the city seemed intermina-

ble. It took a monumental effort on her part to respond
rationally to Paul's attempts at conversation, and she
wasn't sure how successful she was being. He gave her
some very strange looks.

"My editor is a real bitch," she offered by way of an
excuse. "Absolutely, totally unreasonable."

"She must be," Paul said dryly. "Ah, here we are," he
added, the cab pulling up in front of the gleaming con-
crete-and-glass skyscraper that housed her publisher's
offices. "Are you sure you don't want me to come along
and protect you?"

"No! Mmm, I'll deal with her myself. See you later."
Marcy opened the door and scrambled out of the cab.
Reaching the entrance, she turned and waved, hoping
he'd take that as a signal to leave. Once inside, she sat
down on a chair in the lobby and forced herself to wait.
It would be the last straw if she came out of the building, only to find Paul and his taxi still there.

Ten minutes later she cautiously emerged and
breathed a sigh of relief. Paul was gone. It took her another ten minutes to find an empty taxi, but finally one
stopped and she climbed in, giving the bored-looking
driver Linda's address.

After an arduous trek through the city's congested
streets, Marcy reached her cousin's apartment building. She was standing in the lobby in front of the locked
elevator, wondering how to get up to the tenth floor
without giving Linda warning that she was here, when

a young woman with five dogs in tow burst through the street door.

"Be careful," she warned Marcy as she inserted her key into the lock, "the little beagle with the sweet expression bites."

Marcy eyed the dogs warily and followed the woman and her charges onto the elevator.

"Gawd!" the woman gasped. "What a hell of a way to make a living! Don't ever take a job walking dogs," she told Marcy. "The pay's awful and the clientele's worse."

"I won't." Marcy edged away from a hairy beast who was beginning to sniff at her ankles.

The elevator came to a halt at the third floor. "Excuse me," the woman muttered. "I get rid of two of the little brutes here." She rushed out, trailed by her yapping entourage.

To Marcy's relief, the elevator continued to the tenth floor with no more stops. She emerged into the dimly lighted hallway, checked the numbers on the doors and quickly located her cousin's apartment. She rang the bell and waited.

She was about to ring again when the door opened to reveal her cousin. Marcy saw Linda first pale to alabaster, then flush a fiery red.

Fear, Marcy decided. Fear and guilt. She felt sorry for her cousin, but things had gone too far to be hushed up any longer. And Stephanie was not going to let the subject of her birth mother drop.

"Hello, Linda." Marcy gave her what she hoped was a reassuring smile. "May I come in?"

"Well . . ." Linda's voice wavered. "Actually, I was about to go out."

"I think it would be best if we could talk now. It's important." Marcy didn't intend to let Linda play a stalling game. She wanted to get this over, tie up the loose ends and get on with her life.

"Then I guess you'd better come in," Linda said, gesturing with a hand that shook. "What is so important that it can't wait until later?"

"Not what, *who*. A teenager named Stephanie Brockton—the baby you had fifteen years ago," Marcy said bluntly, seeing no reason to fence. The quicker the cards were laid on the table, the closer they would be to playing out this little game.

Linda turned chalk white and sank onto the beige sofa. "All this time . . . I think I've always known it would come out, sooner or later. Although in my heart I'd hoped . . ." She bit her lip. "But I knew my time had finally run out when Pam called last week. . . ."

"Pam?"

"Yeah, dear old Pam and her causes. She said you'd just been reunited with the daughter you'd given up for adoption and that she was organizing a welcome-to-the-family shower. She asked if I wanted to contribute something." Linda's laugh was harsh. "I felt like telling her I'd already contributed the kid. What more did she want? My sanity maybe?" A muscle beside her right eye twitched.

"All these years and no one ever suspected," she went on. "Strange, isn't it? I never thought the Brocktons would be the ones to tell. They promised."

"They kept their word. They were killed last spring in an accident. Stephanie found the adoption papers among their things, and that started her looking for you."

"Dead!" The pupils of Linda's dark eyes widened in horror. "But she can't come here! She can't! The Brocktons had money. Real money. Someone has to be responsible for her. She can't live here!" The words tumbled out in a panic-stricken rush.

Marcy wondered at Linda's terrified reaction. It didn't make a great deal of sense. She could understand embarrassment, even anger that her secret was about to become the family's latest nine-day wonder, but fear?

"Stephanie's a person," she pointed out. "A real person who's hurting."

"She's hurting!" Linda's voice broke. "Sometimes it seems like *I* haven't had a moment's peace since I found out I was pregnant with her. Hell!" She clasped her shaking hands. "I wouldn't even admit to myself what had happened until it was too late to get an abortion."

"But why use *my* identity?" Marcy asked. "Why not use your own name?"

Linda's face reflected utter misery. "Because I didn't know what else to do. When I couldn't hide the pregnancy anymore, I called a crisis center. They said that at six and a half months it was too late to do anything but have the child and put it up for adoption. They said that if I was eighteen, I wouldn't need my parents' permission to do it. And you were eighteen."

"You mean you never told your mother?" Marcy asked in disbelief.

"Tell her? Tell her what? That my stepfather had been sexually abusing me since I was eight years old? That her darling second husband was the father of my baby? I may have been only fifteen, but I wasn't stupid. I knew he'd deny it, and she'd believe him. The way she always believed him." Linda's tone was flat, hopeless.

Hardly able to believe what she had just heard, Marcy stared at her cousin; the appalling confession burned its way into her mind.

"Are you saying that Uncle Bert sexually abused you?" she asked, carefully repeating her cousin's words, somehow wanting to believe that she'd misunderstood.

"Yes! Yes! Yes!" Linda wrapped her arms around herself and rocked back and forth, visibly in agony. "He abused me and abused me and finally got me pregnant!" Her voice rose hysterically. "I was so young and scared. That son of a bitch even managed to convince me that it was all my fault. That if I told anyone, I'd be sent away because I was bad."

She laughed bitterly. "Instead, I ran away. But first I stole your identification out of your father's desk, when we were visiting one Sunday afternoon. I had copies made and returned the originals. Then I studied the Adoption columns in the Chicago papers. You know the kind. Where people who want to adopt advertise for pregnant fools like me. Anyway, I must have responded to half a dozen of them before I found the Brocktons. They seemed to be exactly the kind of parents I'd have liked to have had myself." She grimaced. "It was really very easy. I told them I was a college student who didn't want anyone to know. And with your identification to back up my story, they believed me. They paid my living and medical expenses, and when the baby was born, I signed her over to them."

"But didn't your mother ever try to find you? You must have been gone for months." Marcy struggled to understand. "And why didn't the family know?"

Linda smiled cynically. "Nobody knew because my stepfather took great pains to cover everything up. When I ran away, I left a note for him, saying I couldn't stand it anymore and that if he tried to find me, I'd tell anyone who would listen how he'd raped me. I don't know what he told my mother. When I called her after the baby was born and I'd moved in with Grandma,

Mom said that while she was disappointed I was so jealous of her love for Bert that I would tell such horrible lies, she still loved me and forgave me. And that I could come back home anytime I wanted. Do you have any idea how galling it is to be forgiven for being a victim? Anyway, I haven't carried on more than a superficial conversation with my mother ever since."

"For what it's worth, your mother's response is very common," Marcy observed. "Especially among women who are financially and emotionally dependent."

"Yeah, that's what my therapist said. To my mother I was expendable, and Bert wasn't."

"Did you tell Grandma what had happened?"

"I told her about the sexual abuse, but not that there'd been a baby," Linda said, confirming Marcy's suspicion. "You know what her response was?" Linda went on. "She said she was an old woman. That she'd shoot him for me. And God help me—" her cousin grimaced "—I was really tempted to let her do it."

"Personally, I think shooting's too good for him!" Marcy exclaimed. "I'd opt for hanging him by his thumbs, opening a vein and letting him bleed to death, slowly."

"So you believe me?" Linda asked hesitantly.

"Of course I believe you!"

Linda gestured, visibly relieved, and said, "Thanks. It means a lot to me that you understand why I used your identity like that. The therapist I saw afterward helped me to come to terms with what had happened, but I still felt . . . guilty about you, even though you didn't know what I'd done. Afterward I finished high school, went to college, got my teaching degree and then married Edward. . . ." Her voice faded.

"What does Edward think about the situation?" Marcy probed.

"I never told him. Oh, I know I should have," Linda hurried on when Marcy stared at her in disbelief. "But I just couldn't. I know Edward. He's the most wonderful man in the world, but he's absolutely unbending about some things, and this whole mess definitely falls into that category. He'd never understand."

"There's also Stephanie to be considered," Marcy pointed out.

"No." Linda shook her head emphatically. "Not by me. To me she's a living reminder of the hell I endured. And now she's going to destroy the life I've built for myself."

Marcy rubbed her forehead and tried to think. She felt as if she'd walked off the bottom step and, instead of landing on firm ground, had fallen into quicksand. Instead of Stephanie being the product of two kids with more hormones than common sense, she was the result of years of terror. Rather than causing Linda some temporary embarrassment while everyone adjusted to the existence of a daughter, Stephanie really could destroy her mother's present life.

"I guess I should have done what my therapist said and told Edward before we were married," Linda said wearily.

"That's in the past, Linda. You can't change it," Marcy pointed out.

"All I've got is a past, one I'm trying to forget. God, Marcy, I've been so scared! I haven't slept more than a few hours at a stretch since Pam called."

Marcy tried to think, but couldn't. She felt as if she, too, were being sucked into the vortex of emotion that was swirling around the room.

"When are you going to tell him?" Now Linda's voice was a thin thread of sound.

"Him?" Marcy stared blankly at her cousin.

"Edward. My husband." Linda's voice cracked.

Marcy shifted restlessly from one foot to the other, fighting a feeling of being suffocated by the weight of Linda's anguish and despair. She had to get out of here.

"*When*, dammit!" Linda's sudden shout made Marcy jump. "Don't play games with me. I have to know!"

"I have absolutely no intention of running to Edward with anything. Not now or at any time in the future," Marcy said defensively.

"You don't have to go to him and you know it. All you have to do is tell someone, anyone, what you figured out, and in a family our size it'll only be a matter of time until someone tells him. For his own good, you understand," she said, mimicking one of their great-aunt's perennial excuses for meddling in other people's affairs.

"I need to think," Marcy said. "Alone."

"But—"

"I'll call you later."

"Thinking doesn't help. I've done nothing but think ever since Pam called, and it hasn't changed a single thing. Not one damn thing. The facts didn't miraculously arrange themselves into a more acceptable pattern. And they never will." Linda began to weep in quiet, hopeless little gasps that made Marcy want to sit down and cry with her.

"Linda, I promise I'll call you later, but right now I have to think. Goodbye." Marcy hurried to the door, half afraid that Linda might try to stop her, but she didn't. As Marcy closed the door, Linda was still sitting on the sofa, arms wrapped around her waist, rocking back and forth in utter misery.

This time Marcy ignored the elevator, preferring to run down the ten flights of stairs, hoping the exercise would burn away some of the seething emotions coursing through her. It didn't. She arrived in the lobby out of breath, still burdened with a mass of unresolved feelings.

She hurried out of the building and hailed a cruising taxi. She needed a quiet, anonymous place where she could think, and the only spot that immediately came to mind was Central Park. Marcy settled back in her seat and stared blindly in front of her. Within minutes, the cabbie deposited her at the entrance to the park, with an injunction not to stray off the beaten paths because it wasn't safe, not even in broad daylight.

Marcy walked until she found an empty bench and sat down. She leaned back, barely registering the sharp pressure of a broken slat that dug into her spine.

Several lunchtime joggers ran by, followed by a pair of young women, each pushing a baby carriage. On the bench to her right, an old man was reading a dog-eared paperback, and across from him a woman in a wheelchair was tossing popcorn to the pigeons. Everything seemed normal. Innocuous. Just as Linda had always seemed normal. But behind that calm front had lurked the terrible story of Linda's past. Marcy bit her lip. Probably every one of these pleasant, contented-looking people around her had dealt with tragedy and betrayal. They'd all learned to cope, and Linda would, too.

But at what cost? What price would she be forced to pay? Her peace of mind? Certainly. Her husband? Maybe. One thing was certain. Linda's life would never be the same again. Not only that, but their whole extended family would in all likelihood be ripped apart. Marcy had had far too much experience dealing with sexual abuse not to know that some members of the family would believe Linda, while others would choose to believe her stepfather's denials. The two groups would polarize, and organizing family gatherings would be tricky.

And where would Stephanie fit into all this? The girl's tear-stained face seemed to float before her. Linda wasn't going to welcome her. After all, she was a living reminder of everything her cousin wanted to forget. That might possibly change at some point in the future, but again, it might not. Especially not if Edward reacted negatively. For the present, at least, Stephanie would be emphatically rejected, at a time when she desperately needed both love and acceptance.

And how would Stephanie feel on finding out that she was the result of a rape? Marcy winced. That knowledge might well do a great deal of damage to the girl's sense of self-worth. And if the family did split into opposing camps, Stephanie would be bound to suffer. Blaming the victim was a game that a lot of otherwise normal people played, sometimes without seeming to be aware they were doing it.

Marcy shifted restlessly on the hard bench. The truth was going to cause horrendous problems for Stephanie, Linda and Edward—and the rest of the family, as well. But if she didn't tell the truth, then she could kiss goodbye to her election as chair of the Psychology Department. Her phone calls over the past week had convinced her that several of her sanctimonious colleagues wouldn't vote for her if they thought Stephanie was hers. And there was no way she could get elected without at least some of their votes.

Dammit, she thought, frustrated. It just wasn't fair. She'd worked hard for that promotion. Not only did she deserve it, but she'd do a far better job at it than Joe Abernathy, who'd never had an original thought in his life.

Too upset to sit still any longer, Marcy got to her feet and began to walk, blindly following the path.

Think, she ordered herself. *Find an answer to all this, some solution that will tie up all the loose ends without strangling anyone in the process.* But try as she might, Marcy couldn't come up with anything even vaguely approaching a solution.

She finally faced the obvious. Stephanie, Linda and Edward's needs were best served by not letting the truth come out, by maintaining the story that Linda had fabricated all those years ago. On the other hand, Marcy's needs would best be served by telling the plain, unvarnished truth.

But just denying that Stephanie was her daughter wouldn't work. She'd been doing that all along, and no one had believed her. No, in order to be believed, she'd have to produce indisputable evidence—the proof Daniel had supplied. There was no other way to establish her own innocence.

Marcy stared blankly ahead. What would be the consequences if she were to keep the whole affair secret? She considered the idea for the first time. For starters, she'd lose her chance for the chair, but her job would still be safe. She had tenure, so they couldn't fire her for any but the most extreme reasons. And an illegitimate child didn't qualify as extreme by any normal person's standards.

Several of her very straitlaced colleagues might snub her, but that didn't really matter. In fact, it might well be a blessing in disguise. Small-minded people had never held any appeal for her. Her friends would be supportive. They'd already proved that. She remembered the many warm, encouraging phone calls she'd received before she'd left the university.

There would be a few embarrassing moments at the next family gathering while everyone adjusted to the idea, but her parents would support her, and the rest of the family loved her and would extend that love to Stephanie. In fact, judging by what Linda had said, Pam was already organizing the welcome.

And how would Paul fit in? Almost from the first time she'd kissed him, she'd asked herself how much of what he felt for her was tied to who she was, and how much to the person he thought she was—Stephanie's mother. If she claimed Stephanie as her daughter, she'd never have to find out. It was an incredibly seductive thought. She could simply enjoy what he felt and not worry about reasoning why.

Would it be wrong to do that? If she had to put up with the negative consequences of claiming Stephanie as her daughter, why shouldn't she take advantage of one of the few benefits? She loved Paul. What was wrong with accepting everything he was willing to give her?

Her conscience, however, was busily pointing out that that didn't make any difference. A lie was a lie, and any relationship founded on such a shaky basis would eventually collapse.

Marcy emerged from the relative quiet of the park to find herself on a crowded sidewalk. Confused, she gazed around, trying to find a landmark. She had no idea where she was. She leaned against a telephone pole and peered up and down the crowded street, looking for a taxi.

Five minutes later, she gave the driver the name of her hotel, sat back and tried to organize her thoughts. She had to make a decision. In favor of Stephanie—or of the chair?

10

MARCY CROSSED THE LOBBY and was about to enter one of the elevators when she realized that she didn't know which button to push. Taking a deep, steadying breath, she turned and approached the front desk.

Ten minutes later she had signed the register and received her key. The trip to the seventeenth floor seemed to take only seconds, and Marcy exited the elevator with another woman, who hurried into a room two doors down.

Marcy wasn't in such a rush. Much as she wanted to see Paul, she still hadn't decided what she was going to say—to do. She stared at the delicate table in the foyer with its huge bouquet of fresh flowers.

If she opted to claim Stephanie, she'd lose the chance for the chair, but would gain a daughter—a thoroughly nice girl whom she was already very fond of. Marcy had no doubt that she'd come to love her in time, as she already loved Stephanie's uncle.

And if she were Stephanie's mother, she'd have an unassailable excuse to visit Boston whenever she wanted. To see Paul whenever she wanted.

Becoming the chair of her department paled into insignificance compared with being Paul's lover. Paul was a vital, totally fascinating man who intrigued and enthralled her on every level of her being. While the position of chair appealed to her intellect, its only emotional appeal would lie in the sense of satisfaction and accomplishment at having achieved it.

Marcy briefly closed her eyes; a sense of peace stole over her. She made her decision. She'd claim Stephanie, go for the emotional fulfillment, and continue to get her career satisfaction the way she had for the past nine years, through teaching and research. She hurried down the hall toward Room 1709.

She wanted to see Paul. Now. To touch him, make love with him before he left for his meeting with the consultant. She glanced at her watch. Only three hours had passed since he'd dropped her off!

Her excitement rising, she inserted the plastic strip into the lock, but the door was pulled open as she started to push, and Marcy found herself staring at Paul.

"Room service?" He grinned.

She gave him a slow smile. "You should be so lucky." She stepped inside, closed the door behind her, then leaned back.

"I already am." He looked down into her face, searching for some sign of the strain she'd been under earlier. He couldn't find any. She seemed calmer now, as if the source of the stress had been removed.

He reached out and traced her cheek with a forefinger, reveling in the soft, velvety texture. It was as if a rose had suddenly been imbued with life.

"You're what?" Marcy asked, feeling the warmth of his caressing fingertip in every fiber of her body.

"Lucky," he said seriously. "I must be to have found you."

Ecstatically happy, Marcy flung herself into his arms. They closed around her with a satisfying promptness and he pulled her closer. She could feel the strength of each muscle in his chest, feel the heat pouring from him. It was as if she were being drawn into a world that held only Paul and herself. A world where the ugly realities of life had no place.

She swallowed and her stomach twisted in anticipation as she remembered the feel of his lips against her own. A shudder of longing shook her. She wanted Paul, wanted him in the most elemental way. Talking could come later, she thought muzzily. Now was the time for actions, not words. "I want you," she said. "I want to make love with you. I want—"

His mouth cut her off in midsentence with a rough hunger that echoed her own need. She could feel the hard wall of his chest pushing against her breasts and the strength of his arms as he held her against him.

Relishing the sensation, Marcy splayed her hands across his back, feeling the warmth of his skin seep through the crisp cotton of his shirt. He was so solid. She sighed rapturously, and snuggled even closer.

"Do you have any idea what you do to me when you do that?" he muttered.

"On a guess, I'd say the same things you do to me."

"You make me feel as if I'm ten feet tall, and omnipotent into the bargain. As if anything were possible."

"Now that's an idea that opens some interesting avenues of research."

Pushing her fingers through his crisp hair, she shivered slightly as the silky strands caressed her fingertips. Tugging his head down, she placed a quick kiss against his mouth, whereupon he swung her off her feet.

"I'm always ready to lend myself to scientific research."

Marcy squeaked in surprise and hastily grabbed at his neck. "What are you doing?" Her shoes slipped off her feet and landed on the thick carpet.

"I'm carrying you off to bed." He turned sideways to maneuver her through the bedroom door. He smelled so good, she thought, taking a deep breath of the heady aroma of soap, cologne and other less easily identifiable scents.

"Until I met you, I never knew that modern men were strong enough to carry a woman anywhere." She nuzzled the raspy skin under his chin, smiling inwardly as his jaw muscles corded in reaction.

"I didn't know it, either," he confided on a husky chuckle that dropped into the pit of her stomach and churned up her emotions. "I've never tried before. Tell you what, if I throw my back out, you can walk on it for me. Like they do in Oriental movies."

"I'm a psychologist, not a physical therapist." Her grip tightened as he flopped onto the bed, and lay back against the thick satin comforter, with Marcy still clutched firmly in his arms.

Moving deliberately, she ground one hip against him, smiling in satisfaction when his body stiffened.

"Marcy!" he gasped.

"Mmm?" She began to nibble on the lobe of one ear. It tasted salty. She caught it between her teeth and bit lightly, giggling at his reaction.

"You have a perverted sense of humor." He pushed her gently onto her back and crouched over her. "And do you know what happens to people like that?"

"They starve." Marcy giggled again. "There really isn't much call for torturers these days. Modern society uses computers to drive people crazy."

"You don't need a computer to drive me mad." Paul gave her a wolfish smile that sent a surge of adrenaline through her. "All you have to do is touch me."

"You'll have to be more precise. What do I have to touch to drive you mad?" She braced her heels against the thick comforter to give herself greater leverage, then pushed upward against his chest. Caught by surprise, he fell sideways; now Marcy was the one on top.

"For example—" she grinned at him "—what do kisses do to you?" She placed one exactly in the center of his chin. "Maybe it takes a little more to turn you on?" She tugged up his shirt to expose his broad chest and studied the whirls of dark brown hair that covered it. Fascinated, she leaned forward and traced the pattern with the tip of her tongue.

Paul jerked convulsively.

"Aha!" She gave him a smile, exulting in her femininity. "We seem to be getting closer to a definition here. However, I feel a little more substantive research is needed."

She deftly pulled off his tie before unbuttoning his shirt and pushing the edges apart, then unbuckled his belt and slowly unzipped his pants, brushing her fingers provocatively against his manhood, which was straining against his white shorts.

"Your research is about to become X-rated!" Paul gasped.

"Not with all these clothes you've got on, it won't," Marcy said. "A person can't even get to you."

"If that's your only problem..." He slid free and stood up.

Marcy rocked back on her heels, watching in breathless fascination as he stripped off his clothes, carelessly tossing them aside until he stood naked in front of her. Her eyes skittered upward and became entangled in the hot blaze of desire in his gaze. She swayed toward him.

"If I had too many clothes on before, then you're certainly overdressed now." He unbuttoned her blouse with fingers made clumsy with haste and pushed it over her shoulders. Her bra quickly followed.

The cool air of the bedroom brushed over her skin, making her shiver.

"Poor Marcy," he murmured. "Don't worry. I'll warm you up." He nuzzled the sensitive indentation behind her ear, then strung kisses along her collarbone, pausing to lick the tiny hollow at the base of her neck.

If she grew any warmer, she'd be in danger of going up in flames, Marcy thought dreamily, seeing everything through a golden haze. Her excitement seemed to be intensifying her response to him. Everything about Paul seemed larger than life, the whole picture sharper. She found the experience intoxicating.

Paul loomed over her, and Marcy put her hands flat against his chest, first rubbing her palms down to his waist, then back up to his shoulders. She could feel the ripple of his muscles as he stirred restlessly beneath her exploring movements. She flexed her fingers, digging them into the firm flesh. A smile curved her lips at his instinctive response. Somehow, being intensely aware of him didn't seem nearly so disturbing when she knew the feeling was mutual.

Slowly her hand drifted lower until it brushed a second time against his hot length; her fingers tentatively tightened around him.

"Marcy!" His voice was a hoarse whisper.

"Don't you like it?" She peered up through her lashes.

"If I like it much more, there won't be any more. And anyway, you're still dressed." He reached down and unzipped her slacks, then pulled them and her panties over her hips.

His raspy breathing suddenly sounded loud in the hush of the bedroom. "You're the most beautiful thing I've ever seen," he muttered. "A perfect pastel study." His fingers traced her waistline, then moved down over her belly.

"Paul. Kiss me." She tugged at his broad shoulders. "Now!"

He lowered his head, stopping a scant inch away. His breath warmed her skin for a fraction of a second, then his lips brushed hers. His mouth was warm and inviting, but she wanted much more than this provocative teasing. She wanted to be closer, to feel Paul's weight pressing into her body, to absorb the movement of his muscles with her flesh, not with her eyes.

Marcy wrapped her arms around his neck and eagerly lifted her head for his kisses.

To her delight, he responded quickly. His mouth closed over hers, then his tongue slid along her bottom lip. His tongue aggressively pushed forward and she opened her lips to welcome him. Her fingers inched up his neck to tangle in his short hair and she began to massage his scalp, but the crisp texture of his hair only heightened her awareness of him, shattering her patience. She wanted to experience him totally, from the exact taste of his hot, seeking tongue to the throbbing length of his manhood deep within her.

She tugged at his hair and, when he lifted his head, demanded, "Let's make love."

He blinked as if trying to bring her into focus, then chuckled unexpectedly. "I thought that's what we were doing."

"You know what I mean." She buried her face against his neck, lightly biting the throbbing vein near his collarbone.

"Don't do that!" he gasped. "I'm trying to—"

"You don't have to try." She gently licked the spot, and the taste of salt flooded her senses.

Cupping her chin with strong fingers, he stared into her face for a long moment.

She could warm herself by the blaze in his eyes, she thought fancifully. They seemed to glow with the force of his emotions.

Finally, as if satisfied by what he saw, he moved over her once more. His knee aggressively parted her thighs, and he slipped between her legs.

"You're so very beautiful," he crooned. His hand slipped between her legs, finding and probing her moistness.

Marcy moved in response to his tongue, brushing her breasts against his hair-roughened chest. The contact excited her unbearably, and she wrapped her arms around his back to hold him closer.

Carefully positioning himself, he slowly thrust forward, giving her body time to adjust.

Marcy flung back her head and, digging her heels into the slick satin comforter, pushed upward, totally engulfing his burning length in her own hot flesh. She clenched her teeth in reaction to the sensation that spiraled through her.

"That's right." Paul's voice seemed to come from a distance, even though his lips were scorching the sensitive skin on her neck. "Feel it," he muttered. "Feel what I feel."

"Yes," she gasped, barely aware of what he was saying. Her own needs were too great. She grasped his lean hips and pulled him down again.

He began to move. Slowly at first, then with more speed; the sensations he was generating seemed to devour both of them. Finally they overwhelmed her, pulling her into a whirlpool of eroticism that totally blotted out everything but the necessity to wring every last nuance from the experience.

She was so caught up in her own reaction that she barely noticed Paul's body stiffen in release, but closed her arms around him. She wanted to hold him, never to let him go.

She trailed her fingers over his back while she tried to think. It wasn't easy. For one thing, she didn't want to think. She wanted to feel, to savor the afterglow of their lovemaking. But she needed to tell him that she was going to claim Stephanie and she needed to do it now. She steeled herself to tell him the truth. The whole, ugly truth.

"Paul?"

"Mmm?" He rolled onto his side and gathered her against his chest.

"About Stephanie . . ." She paused, trying to decide how to phrase it.

"You mean about her being your daughter?" His breath warmed the skin behind her ear.

"It would seem she is my daughter. You see—"

"You won't be sorry." Paul's grip tightened. "I knew the woman I loved couldn't deny her own child. Not for long."

Marcy tilted her head and stared at him in shock. "What did you say?"

Paul stopped nuzzling her neck long enough to ask, "Which what? The what about how much I love you?"

Marcy searched his earnest face, almost afraid to believe what he was saying. She had wanted to hear it so badly that she was almost afraid she'd imagined the words.

"You love me?" she repeated.

"From the top of your silky head—" he dropped a kiss on her hair "—to the bottom of your feet and all the interesting little bits and pieces in between. Marcy... marry me and I'll do my damnedest to make you happy."

Marcy felt the muscles in his arms clench. Tension was tightening her own muscles, too, making them feel like overstretched wires.

Paul had said he loved her; he wouldn't lie about something like that. Not Paul. But her earlier doubts returned to haunt her. He thought she was Stephanie's mother, he knew Stephanie wanted her, and he wanted Stephanie to be happy.

Marcy closed her eyes, and uncertainty swept through her. He hadn't proposed until she'd claimed Stephanie.

She tried to rationalize her fears. People loved each other for all kinds of reasons, and if Paul's wasn't precisely what she would have preferred, he still wanted to marry her. And he said he loved her. Surely that was enough to base a marriage on?

But if his proposal of marriage had been prompted by the assumption that she was Stephanie's mother...

What harm could it do to let him go on believing it? She wasn't taking anything from anyone else. It wasn't as if he were going to fall in love with Linda. And it wasn't as if Linda would be cheated out of a role in Stephanie's life, because Linda most emphatically wanted no part of the girl. Whom would she be hurting if she let Paul go on thinking she really was Stephanie's mother?

Herself. And Paul. Ultimately, their relationship. So what kind of life could they build? What kind of future could they have?

She answered her own question. Lies had no place in a marriage. On the other hand, if she told him the truth, she might lose him. She felt a sudden chill of dread. But if she allowed the lie to stand and he found out, she might still lose him, and his respect into the bargain.

"Marcy?" Paul's voice sounded slightly strained. "You haven't said you'll marry me. If it's your career you're worried about, we can work something out. Even if we can only have weekends together, that's better than not having you at all."

"It's not the job," she said slowly. "I could easily teach here. There are several excellent colleges in Boston. And there's always a demand for volunteer counselors."

"Then if it's not your career that's making you hesitate, it must be me."

"No," Marcy hastened to assure him. "You have to know that I love you. You're everything I ever wanted in a man."

"Then why do I hear the echo of a resounding 'but' hanging in the air?"

Marcy closed her eyes and gathered her courage. She badly wanted to say there was no 'but,' that what had really been worrying her was her career. She just couldn't bring herself to utter the lie and sell out her long-held beliefs for short-term gains.

"There is a 'but' and it's the truth." She forced the words out. "I do intend to claim Stephanie as my daughter, but the fact is that I didn't give birth to her."

Paul propped himself on one elbow and stared at her. "Tell me about it," he finally said.

"Her mother is my cousin Linda. She pilfered my identification and forged my signature on the release of custody form," Marcy said flatly. "I had a friend in the Criminology Department compare the signatures with those on my mother's Christmas cards. He called me day before yesterday with the results."

Paul frowned. "But why did she do that? Why *your* identity?"

"Because she was underage, I was already eighteen, and she had access to my papers. And as for the other why..." Marcy sighed. "Because she was scared out of her mind and desperate into the bargain. And let me tell you, sixteen years haven't improved her perspective on the situation."

"That's why you came to New York, of course. To see her. So why all the games about your editor?"

"Because I didn't feel I had the right to tell you anything until I'd had a chance to talk to Linda."

"And what Linda said made you decide to claim Stephanie?"

Marcy stared at her hands for a moment, taking heart from the fact that he hadn't withdrawn. Finally she said, "Yes. Linda was sexually abused by her stepfather, and Stephanie is the result."

"Goddammit to hell!"

"So you must see why I can't tell the truth. It would destroy Linda, and Stephanie could never handle it. At least, not at this stage of her life."

"I should say not! Even forgetting your cousin, think how Stephanie would feel if she knew."

"I have."

"There's one aspect of this that worries me." Paul sat up on the edge of the bed. "So far Stephanie's focus has been on getting you to admit that you're her mother."

"Uh-huh?"

"What happens once you admit it?"

Marcy stared at him uncomprehendingly. "What do you mean, what happens? We begin to work out some kind of relationship."

"Perhaps, but knowing my niece, I'll give you odds that her next questions will be, 'Who's my father?'"

Marcy clicked her tongue in frustration. "I really am slow on the uptake today, aren't I? That never even occurred to me."

"You've had a lot on your mind." He walked around the bed, scooped her into his arms, and carried her to one of the chairs next to the window. He sat down with her in his lap.

Marcy snuggled closer. "I could get really attached to this, 'You Tarzan, me Jane' routine of yours."

"Hmm, after we get this mess sorted out, I'll give you the next installment in the primitive man's handbook. First, though, what are we going to do about Stephanie's father?"

Marcy's spirits soared. He'd said "we" twice. "I could say that . . . that I didn't know who the father was."

Paul gave her a wry look. "No one who knows you is going to believe that you hop in and out of so many beds that you can't name your own kid's father."

Marcy savored his assessment of her character for a minute, then said, "Well . . . Suppose we say he's dead. That he died before I even knew I was pregnant."

Paul frowned consideringly. "Better, but she's still going to want to meet his family."

"Hmm. How about if we say he's an orphan?"

"Clichéd. She'd never believe it."

"And if she doesn't believe it . . ."

"She'll keep digging."

"And she just might uncover the whole ugly mess," Marcy said.

"Stephan," Paul said suddenly. "We'll use Stephan. He won't mind. He was a great guy."

"Fine by me. Who's Stephan?"

"My older brother. He died of leukemia six months before Stephanie was adopted. That's why she's called Stephanie."

Marcy considered his idea. It was better than anything she had to offer. "We could say that I wasn't ready for marriage at the time, then Stephan got ill and I didn't want to worry him, and that was why your sister adopted her. Paul, your idea's inspired," she said slowly. "It takes care of all the loose ends."

"Not all of them." Paul's face was suddenly set in serious lines. "There's still the matter of my proposal of marriage."

Marcy slowly licked her lower lip; she tried to think of some way to allow him to withdraw his offer honorably. She couldn't bear for him to marry her simply because he'd already asked and he thought she expected it now.

"Maybe we ought to think about it for a while," she said at last.

"I'm fast coming to the opinion that you think too much," he said shortly. "I love you. You say you love me. You say you're willing to relocate to Boston. So what's the problem . . . Stephanie?"

Marcy looked up and finally voiced her one remaining doubt. "Are you asking me to marry you because you want a mother for Stephanie?"

"A mother…" He stared at her in shock. "Good God, woman, I love my niece, but there is no way that I would ever saddle myself with an unwanted wife just to make her happy. I want to marry you to make *me* happy."

"Really?"

"Positively." His arms tightened around her. "You're everything I ever wanted in a woman, and a few things I didn't even realize I wanted. Now, will you marry me?"

"Yes, yes, yes!" Marcy punctuated each yes with a kiss. "I'll marry you just as soon as it can be arranged."

"And you'll move to Boston."

"And I'll move to Boston."

"And you'll learn to play chess."

"And I'll learn to play chess."

"And we'll have four children."

"And you'll quit while you're ahead."

"All right, we'll table that proposal for the moment." Paul's mouth hovered an inch above hers. "How about making love morning, noon and night?"

"Now that's a plan I can wholeheartedly endorse." Marcy pulled his head down to meet her lips.

$\mathcal{O}$*nce upon a time...*

There was the best romance series in all the land—Temptation

You loved the heroes of REBELS & ROGUES. Now discover the magic and fantasy of romance. *Pygmalion, Cinderella* and *Beauty and the Beast* have an enduring appeal—and are the inspiration for Temptation's exciting new yearlong miniseries, LOVERS & LEGENDS. Bestselling authors including Gina Wilkins, Glenda Sanders, JoAnn Ross and Tiffany White reweave these classic tales—with lots of sizzle! One book a month, LOVERS & LEGENDS continues in May 1993 with:

#441 THE VIRGIN AND THE UNICORN
Kelly Street
(Unicorns)

Live the fantasy....

LL5

HARLEQUIN®

Temptation

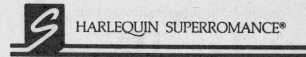

HARLEQUIN SUPERROMANCE®

HARLEQUIN SUPERROMANCE NOVELS WANTS TO INTRODUCE YOU TO A DARING NEW CONCEPT IN ROMANCE...

WOMEN WHO DARE!
Bright, bold, beautiful...
Brave and caring, strong and passionate...
They're women who know their own minds
and will dare anything...
for love!

One title per month in 1993, written by popular Superromance authors, will highlight our special heroines as they face unusual, challenging and sometimes dangerous situations.

Next month, time and love collide in:
#549 PARADOX by Lynn Erickson
Available in May wherever Harlequin Superromance novels are sold.

HARLEQUIN®

THE TAGGARTS OF TEXAS!

Harlequin's Ruth Jean Dale brings you
THE TAGGARTS OF TEXAS!

Those Taggart men—strong, sexy and hard to resist...

You've met Jesse James Taggart in FIREWORKS!
Harlequin Romance #3205 (July 1992)

And Trey Smith—he's THE RED-BLOODED YANKEE!
Harlequin Temptation #413 (October 1992)

And the unforgettable Daniel Boone Taggart in SHOWDOWN!
Harlequin Romance #3242 (January 1993)

Now meet Boone Smith and the Taggarts who started it all—
in LEGEND!
Harlequin Historical #168 (April 1993)

Read all the Taggart romances!
Meet all the Taggart men!

Available wherever Harlequin Books are sold.

Where do you find hot Texas nights, smooth Texas charm and dangerously sexy cowboys?

Crystal Creek

AMARILLO BY MORNING

Show time—Texas style!

Everybody loves a cowboy, and Cal McKinney is one of the best. So when designer Serena Davis approaches this handsome rodeo star, the last thing Cal expects is a business proposition!

CRYSTAL CREEK reverberates with the exciting rhythm of Texas. Each story features the rugged individuals who live and love in the Lone Star State. And each one ends with the same invitation...

Y'ALL COME BACK...REAL SOON!

Don't miss *AMARILLO BY MORNING* by Bethany Campbell. Available in May wherever Harlequin books are sold.